Sarah and Katie

by DORI WHITE

Illustrations by
Trina Schart Hyman

SCHOLASTIC BOOK SERVICES
NEW YORK • TORONTO • LONDON • AUCKLAND • SYDNEY • TOKYO

Text copyright © 1972 by Dori White. Pictures copyright © 1972 by Trina Schart Hyman. This edition is published by Scholastic Book Services, a division of Scholastic Magazines, Inc., by arrangement with Harper & Row, Publishers, Inc.

1st printing .... December 1972

Printed in the U.S.A.

Sarah and Katie

For My Mother

Contents

1 / New Girl in School

"Katie, please hurry," Sarah begged.

"I'm hurrying as fast as I can." Katie's stubby yellow braids bobbed as she panted alongside Sarah. "My legs aren't as long as yours."

It wasn't really necessary to run. The two girls, who had been walking to school together since the first grade, had started nearly half an hour early on this important day. In her left hand, Sarah carried a folder. In the folder was the play that she and Katie had written together for the sixth-grade Thanksgiving Play contest.

"I'm glad it's such a nice day," Sarah said, trying to slow down for Katie. "It makes me almost sure we'll win."

1

"I don't see what the weather has to do with our winning," Katie gasped.

"My father says that sunshine means good luck."

"Then it's good luck for everyone else, too. Sarah, I can't hurry anymore. My side hurts. I'll bet Miss Lane isn't there yet, anyway."

"Of course she'll be there," Sarah said, but she stopped to let Katie rest. The playground was just across the street. "Teachers always come early."

"Not Miss Lane," Katie said stubbornly. "She's late lots of times. I saw her yesterday, running in at the very last minute before the bell rang." Suddenly, she caught Sarah's arm. "Listen. Do you hear what I hear?" Heavy footsteps—boy's footsteps—pounded along the side street. "I'll bet it's Danny Wade," Katie whispered.

"Just our luck!" Sarah looked around for a place to hide. She was afraid of Danny Wade, who was the biggest boy in school, although he was only in the sixth grade. She clutched the play more tightly. It would be just like Danny to grab it and tear it. "Come on," she said, and seized Katie's hand.

They had barely begun to scramble up a grassy bank where there were bushes to hide behind, when Danny reached the corner. Sarah was sure he saw them. His eyes gleamed, his face grew more sullen, and his stride lengthened. He ran straight at them.

"Run, Katie!" Sarah screamed, and jumped down from the bank, stretching her long legs over the sidewalk, and keeping a tight grip on the folder. As she leaped the curb, she heard Katie panting behind her, and took a quick glance over her shoulder. Danny had nearly caught Katie. "Faster!" she cried.

"I can't," Katie gasped, and then she gave a despairing, "Oh-h-h," and stopped short. Sarah faltered. Danny galloped past Katie as if she weren't there. As he caught up to Sarah, his shoulder hit hers, knocking her off balance. Her arms flew out wildly, she skidded, and then sat down hard in the middle of the street. The folder leaped from her grasp and the papers inside caught in the breeze, scattering like white leaves.

"Our play! Oh, how mean," Sarah wailed. "Katie, did he hurt you?"

Katie was rapidly gathering up papers. "He tore my sash," she said in a voice that sounded as if she might cry. "I don't know what Mama will say. I only have two school dresses."

"Oh, Katie." Sarah picked up the nearest pages and scrambled to her feet.

3

"I think we've got them all," Katie said. "They aren't too dirty."

Katie looked and sounded thoroughly unhappy, and Sarah knew why. It was because of her sash, and her sash mattered because of the Depression. Sarah hated the Depression. It made her feel awful to have three brand-new school dresses with puffed sleeves, while Katie's dresses had rickrack around the bottom to hide where they'd been let down.

"Let me see your sash." She bent over to inspect the spot where Katie's pink slip showed through her brown gingham dress. "It isn't really torn," she said with relief. "It's only pulled out of the seam. Your mother can fix it."

"But I can't go around all day like this." Despairingly, Katie held out the dangling end of the sash, still tied in a bow.

"We could go back to my house," Sarah said. "My mother would mend it for you."

"No." Katie's face took on her stubborn look. "We started to hand our play in early, so let's do it. I'll get a pin someplace." She marched to the curb and sat down. "Do you have the first page, Sarah? I don't."

Sarah sat down beside her and they sorted through the carefully written pages, brushing the

4

dust from them and putting them in order, until the play looked almost as good as new. When they started out again, Katie seemed nearly cheerful, but the fun had gone out of the morning for Sarah. She had thought about the play and dreamed about the play since the contest was first announced by Miss Lane, the beautiful new Auditorium teacher. And now, on the very day they were to hand it in, Danny Wade had spoiled everything. She didn't see why he had to be so mean.

They crossed the playground in silence, giving a wide berth to Danny, who was shooting baskets near the fence. A group of girls were playing hopscotch by the steps, but Sarah and Katie hurried past. Inside, the halls were deserted and smelled of the cleaner that Mr. Scott, the janitor, used. As they mounted the wide steps to the second floor, Sarah's excitement began to return. She loved Auditorium, where they listened to records, and learned folk-dancing, and sometimes put on plays. This year, she was sure, Auditorium was going to be better than ever.

"Don't you *hope* Miss Lane will like our play?" she asked, squeezing Katie's arm.

"I don't see how she can help it," Katie said. "You really write awfully well, Sarah."

Sarah stared at Katie. "You wrote it, too."

"No, I didn't. I had some of the ideas, but you did all the writing."

"You can't write without ideas," Sarah said rather impatiently. Sometimes Katie was almost *too* honest. "It's your play as much as mine."

Katie didn't answer, but her face turned pink, and she looked rather pleased as she pulled open the wide door that led to the auditorium.

The huge room was dim and quiet. Green blinds covered the windows, shutting out the sunlight. A few thin rays crept around the edges of the blinds to fall across the wooden seats that were arranged in ascending rows, exactly like a real theater. In front of the seats, and directly below the stage with its red curtain, stood a tidy, brown desk. Its chair was empty.

"She isn't here," Sarah exclaimed.

She was more disappointed than she liked to admit. It had been her idea to come early and give their play to Miss Lane before school. She thought Miss Lane would be sure to notice them more at that hour than if they waited until seventh period and handed it in with all the others. Sarah wanted Miss Lane to notice them.

"I told you she wouldn't be," Katie said.

"Maybe she's in her office."

"I don't think she'd like us to go back there," Katie said. "I don't think she likes being bothered."

"Katie! She's a teacher."

"Yes, I know," Katie said stubbornly, "but I don't think she likes children much. When Betty Evans fell down and hurt her knee, Miss Lane walked right past her."

"Maybe she didn't see her."

"Betty thought she did." Katie turned toward the door. "Let's go, Sarah. I have to find a pin, and it's getting late. We can hand our play in at Auditorium period."

She pulled at the big door, and Sarah was turning reluctantly to follow, when the backstage door opened, and there was Miss Lane in her pale pink dress, looking unbelievably pretty. She smiled, and Sarah felt almost weak with admiration.

"What is it, girls?" she asked.

Sarah glanced at Katie, and then stepped forward, holding out the folder. "It's our play." Miss Lane looked at her blankly. "For the contest. The Thanksgiving contest."

"Oh," Miss Lane said. "Oh, yes, of course. You're in seventh period, aren't you? Well, thank you very much." She smiled again.

7

"When—?" Sarah asked breathlessly. "When will you say who won, Miss Lane?"

"When? Let's see." Miss Lane lifted her hand to tuck in a brown curl, and Sarah saw a flash of fire on her finger. She was wearing a new ring—a diamond ring! "I'll announce the winners on Friday. Do you think you can wait until then?"

"Oh, yes." Sarah hunted in her mind for words to describe Miss Lane. *Tall and gracious . . . hung with diamonds . . .* "That's a pretty ring," she heard herself saying.

Miss Lane turned as pink as her dress and laughed. "Thank you, dear," she said and, still smiling to herself, went behind the stage and shut the door.

"Isn't she lovely?" Sarah said dreamily.

"She didn't even know who we were!" Katie marched out into the hall. "Come on, Sarah. Let's go."

Sarah ran to catch up. "Oh, Katie, imagine—if we win. We'll get to give our play for the whole school."

"Yes, but if we don't win, we won't be in the program at all. A play is a good idea, I guess, but it's going to leave a lot of people out."

"Oh, Katie!" Katie criticized anything Miss

Lane did, and Sarah couldn't understand why. Miss Lane was the prettiest, sweetest teacher they had ever had at Roseland School. "I'm not going to *think* about being left out," she said. "This is going to be the best Thanksgiving program we ever had, and I couldn't bear not to be in it. I'll bet a lot of parents will come this year, because of the baskets."

Since times were hard that year, and a great many men in Portland were out of work, Mr. Tuttle, the principal of Roseland School, had suggested that admission of a sort be charged for the annual Thanksgiving program. Each child or adult who came would bring some kind of food— apples, or canned fruit, or homemade jam—for the Thanksgiving baskets that were to be given to needy families in the neighborhood.

"My mother says I can make fudge for the baskets," Katie said, as they rounded the corner and came under the steely gaze of Miss Mulkey, their homeroom teacher.

If Sarah and Katie disagreed about Miss Lane, they disagreed even more about Miss Mulkey. Sarah thought she was mean. You didn't dare make the tiniest sound in Miss Mulkey's room, or you'd have to stay after school. Katie said she was a good

9

teacher and really fair. Sarah wasn't sure about that. Once, when Sarah was writing a poem during arithmetic period, Miss Mulkey had taken it away and *kept it*. Sarah didn't call that fair.

"Katherine," she said as the girls approached, "you've torn your sash." Her arms were folded over her thin chest, and her glasses glinted at them severely. Sarah shivered, but Katie walked right up and tipped her head to smile at Miss Mulkey.

"Yes, Miss Mulkey," she said. "If I had a pin, I could fix it."

Sarah held her breath, waiting for Miss Mulkey to ask how the sash had been torn. They wouldn't dare tell her. Everyone said that if you told on Danny Wade, he'd get even. But Miss Mulkey only looked at the sash, set her lips, and disappeared into the room. When she came back a moment later, she held a large safety pin.

"Take Sarah to help you," she said, putting the pin in Katie's hand. "And don't loiter. It's almost time for the bell."

"Thank you, Miss Mulkey," Katie said, and threw Sarah a glance that meant, *See? She isn't so bad*. But Sarah could feel Miss Mulkey's eye boring into her back.

"We'd better hurry," she whispered. It would be

just like Miss Mulkey to punish them if they were late.

The tardy-bell was clanging in the empty halls when they slipped through the homeroom door again, with the sash pinned in place. Danny Wade gave them a dark glance from the back of the room, where he sprawled with his feet in the aisle and his black hair hanging over his face. Sarah quickly turned her head away. Then she almost stopped walking. Miss Mulkey was smiling, and she was smiling at her.

"Take your seat, Sarah," Miss Mulkey said. "I want to introduce our new student to the class."

Sarah saw then that the seat across the aisle from hers was occupied, not by Betty Evans, but by a new girl—a most amazing looking girl, who seemed to be quite aware that every eye in the class was on her, but who didn't look as if she minded a bit. Her dark red hair was longer than any Sarah had ever seen. Most of the girls wore short bobs, and it seemed odd to see the new girl's hair curl right down to the seat behind her. *She's awfully pretty,* Sarah thought. Her face was pale and delicate, and her brows swept across it like—like slender bird wings. But it was her clothes that caused Sarah to stumble into her seat. She wore a blue

11

velvet dress, blue socks, and—*blue slippers*. Exactly like a princess.

Miss Mulkey was still smiling. "This is Melanie Rivers, class," she said. "Melanie has moved to Portland from Hollywood, California, and we'll try to make her feel welcome, won't we, boys and girls?"

She paused. Her smile disappeared as suddenly as if she had swallowed it. "Take out your arithmetic," she ordered, and her voice and look were as severe as ever.

Sarah made more mistakes than usual that morning. Even the play contest was swept from her mind as her eyes strayed again and again to the girl across the aisle. Melanie was from Hollywood! Somehow, Sarah had never thought of ordinary boys and girls living in Hollywood. But maybe Melanie *wasn't* an ordinary girl. Maybe she was a movie star. She was pretty enough.

When the bell rang for lunch, a crowd gathered around Melanie, who smiled and answered questions, and tossed back her heavy hair. Sarah wondered how a new girl could act so natural, and she edged closer, fascinated.

"I don't actually *know* any movie stars," Melanie was saying in her clear voice, "but I've

seen lots and lots of them. Greta Garbo's limousine used to go past our house nearly every morning."

"Greta Garbo," Eddie Barker said scornfully. "Who cares about old Greta Garbo? Did you ever see Tom Mix or Hoot Gibson?"

"Or Rin Tin Tin?" Will Stevens put in eagerly. Melanie flashed her gay smile at Will, who seemed dazed by it. "I've petted Rin Tin Tin," she said. "My uncle knows his trainer, and he took me to see him."

Everyone fell silent, and Sarah herself was awe-struck at actually knowing a girl who had petted the most famous dog in the world. Melanie tossed her hair. "I'm hungry," she said plaintively. "Won't someone show me where the lunch-room is?"

A dozen hands reached for her, and Sarah, who liked walking home at noon, wished she were eating at school. Katie tugged at her arm. "Come *on*, Sarah."

Out on the playground a brisk wind whipped their sweaters, and the bright air smelled unmistakably of autumn. It was a beautiful blue-and-gold day, a wide-awake day, with Mount Hood standing out clear and sharp above the tips of the fir trees, like a huge dish of vanilla ice cream.

"Race you to the fence," Sarah called to Katie, and began to run.

When they had reached the fence, laughing and panting, and had started up the long block to Sarah's house, Katie said, "Do you know what Wanda Wiggins told me? She said Danny Wade didn't even *write* a play. Can you imagine? And she said Eddie and Will gave up on the Indians and wrote about pirates instead. I don't see what pirates have to do with Thanksgiving, do you?"

"It's too bad Melanie didn't come last week," Sarah said. "Now she's missed out on the contest." Katie didn't answer, and after a moment Sarah sighed, "Melanie Rivers. Isn't that the loveliest name? I wish I had a name like that."

"I think it's silly," Katie said shortly. "It sounds like a name in a book."

"But that's what's nice about it," Sarah cried. "And anyway, she didn't *choose* her name."

"I suppose not. But she doesn't have to talk about movie stars all the time."

Sarah was astonished. She stopped and faced her friend. Katie's face was red, and her mouth unhappy. "Katie Donnelly, you're not being fair. Her name isn't her fault, and it isn't her fault if she knows movie stars either."

Katie's face grew redder. "Well, I think she's silly. It's silly to wear a velvet dress to school." She trudged on, her eyes down. "And you're not being fair either, Sarah Abbott. You're only sticking up for her because she's pretty."

"That's not true!"

Katie stared straight ahead, and neither one of them said a word until they reached the brown-shingled house where Sarah lived.

"Shall I pick you up after lunch?" Katie asked grudgingly, when they came to the big fir by Sarah's driveway.

Her tone made Sarah angry. "I don't care whether you do or not," she snapped, and ran up the drive.

2 / The Play Contest

As soon as Sarah reached the back steps, she was sorry for what she'd said, and she ran back to the sidewalk. But Katie had already turned the corner. *She started it,* Sarah thought, but it wasn't a very comforting thought, and she dragged herself into the house, slowly.

Mrs. Abbott, a plump and comfortable looking woman, liked to hear about school, and ordinarily Sarah liked to tell her. When she had just quarreled with her very best friend, however, nothing else seemed important. As she ate her lunch, she told her mother reluctantly about handing in the play, and about the new girl. It didn't help a bit

17

when Mrs. Abbott lifted her hands and laughed, exclaiming, "A velvet dress? In school?"

"Maybe she's rich," Sarah muttered.

Mrs. Abbott stopped laughing. "Or maybe that's what the girls wear in California. Are you watching the clock, Sarah? It's almost time to go back to school."

Sarah was watching the clock, but she was also listening for Katie's RAP-rap-rap at the back door. "I suppose I'd better start back," she murmured, and got up slowly.

"Did you and Katie have a spat?"

Sarah was used to her mother knowing things without being told. She looked at the floor. "I said something mean. And now Katie's mad." She raised her eyes. "I wish I hadn't. It just popped out."

Mrs. Abbott smiled. "We all do that. My goodness, if I had a nickel for everything I've said that I didn't mean, I'd be rich." She patted Sarah's shoulder. "Tell Katie you're sorry, and I'm sure it will be all right."

Sarah wasn't so sure, but as she ran to school—she was so late she had to run—she began to feel much better. When she saw Katie's yellow head in the cluster of children crowding into the sixth-grade room, it seemed the most natural thing in the world to slip her hand into Katie's and squeeze. After a startled moment, Katie squeezed back, and Sarah floated to her seat feeling the special glow that comes from being the first to make up. *Everything is all right now,* she thought.

But it wasn't entirely all right. Later that afternoon, Miss Mulkey asked Sarah to explain to Melanie what they were doing in Language. As she squeezed into Melanie's seat, Sarah saw Katie watching her. It made her uncomfortable, as if by helping Melanie she was being disloyal to Katie. Then she sniffed in delight, and forgot Katie. Melanie was wearing perfume.

Sarah explained softly about workbooks and compositions, and Melanie listened without much interest; but the minute Miss Mulkey turned to the blackboard, she put up her hand and whispered behind it, "What do you do for fun? Do you have any clubs?" Sarah shook her head and frowned warningly, but Melanie only laughed. "We had a club in Hollywood," she said softly. "There were just six of us, and the others were dying to get in."

Sarah glanced uneasily at the back of Miss Mulkey's head. She wanted to ask what kind of a club it was, but she didn't dare, so she talked doggedly

about the workbook. Melanie shrugged, and once more Sarah caught the delightful scent of perfume. *Wait until I tell Katie,* she thought.

She was bursting with talk about Melanie's perfume, Melanie's gold bracelet, and the lace on Melanie's slip; but something about Katie's face as they walked home after school kept her silent. When they reached the big fir, they stopped and looked at each other uncertainly.

"Can you stay awhile?" Sarah asked automatically.

Katie drew a long breath. "I was wrong," she said. "About Melanie, I mean. I shouldn't have said those things when I don't know her yet."

"I don't know her either," Sarah said, feeling that Katie's honesty deserved a return. "But I think she's—well, she's *interesting.*"

Katie nodded, not too happily, and scraped her toe along the sidewalk. "You go ahead and be friends with her if you want to."

"Don't *you* want to be friends?"

Katie looked up. "I'm not sure Melanie wants to be friends with either one of us."

Before Sarah could reply to that, Mrs. Abbott called them in the house to help her make popcorn. "I can't stay very long," Katie said, unbuttoning her sweater. "The baby's been crying a lot at night, and I have to help Mama."

Mrs. Abbott smiled at her. "You must be a big help, Katie. Your mother has her hands full."

"Seven children *do* make a lot of work," Katie said, sounding almost as grown-up as Sarah's mother. "I like babies, but I hope we don't have another right away. Daddy says if people don't start paying their dentist bills pretty soon, he's going to give some of us away. But I don't think he means it."

"I'm sure he doesn't," Mrs. Abbott said, but she sighed and stared into space with a frown. Sarah, who was almost sure that when her mother got that look she was thinking about Hard Times, began to talk very fast about the play contest. "Katie's going to be the little sick girl, Collette," she told her mother, "and I'm going to be the—what do you call it—the one who tells everyone what to do."

"*If* we win," Katie said.

"If you win," Mrs. Abbott echoed. "Don't hope too hard."

"Oh, we won't," Sarah said brightly.

She hadn't told anyone, not even Katie, how much she wanted to win the play contest. They had worked very hard on their play, and she didn't think anyone in the sixth grade was likely to write one much better than hers and Katie's. She wanted to win for the fun of winning, but more than that she had a feeling inside that she and Katie would work harder than anyone else after they won.

Sarah had another reason, too, that she wouldn't have mentioned to anyone because she was rather ashamed of it. Everyone said she was the best writer in her class. Her compositions were almost always chosen to be put up on the bulletin board. She felt she was expected to win, just as Betty Evans was expected to win the art contests. It would be terribly embarrassing if she didn't win.

"This is awfully good popcorn," Katie said, "but I'd better go."

"Take some with you," Mrs. Abbott suggested. "And, Katie, ask your mother if you can come to dinner Friday night. If you win the contest, we'll have a grand celebration. If you lose, we'll call it a consolation dinner."

*   *   *   *

A dozen times in the next three days Sarah was sure the dinner would be a celebration; a dozen times she was equally sure it wouldn't. Everyone in the class wanted to win, and some of them acted as if they already had. Martha Waterhouse and Wanda Wiggins had even promised parts to their best friends. When Martha made excuses to go to Miss Lane's desk during Auditorium period and whisper to her, it made Sarah uneasy.

"Maybe she told them they won," Sarah suggested.

"Of course she didn't," Katie said. "They always act that way. They don't know any more than we do." But her face looked as uncertain as Sarah felt.

When Friday came at last, Sarah awoke to a gray world and a driving rain. Katie phoned to say that her father was driving her to school early, and Mrs. Abbott made Sarah wear her galoshes and carry an umbrella. As Sarah sloshed to school alone, she was dismally certain that nothing good could happen on such a day.

Certainly Miss Mulkey's temper hadn't been improved by the weather. She snapped at Sarah for accidentally squeaking her chalk on the blackboard, and sent Wanda to the hall for passing notes, when Wanda had only been returning an arithmetic paper Katie had dropped. At recess they had to play in the gym with three other classes, and when Danny Wade ran into a smaller boy and knocked him down, Miss Mulkey promptly lined them all up and made them do exercises for the rest of the period.

It isn't fair, Sarah thought as she hopped and clapped to Miss Mulkey's crisp, *"One-*two, *one-*two." *She* hadn't done anything. She stole a look at Danny. He was glowering at Miss Mulkey, and barely moving his arms. *He looks like a tramp,* Sarah thought. She felt much better, however, when she saw Katie looking her way and wriggling a yellow lunch ticket. That meant they would both be eating at school.

The lunchroom seemed even noisier than usual, and most of the noise was coming from two long tables where the sixth graders were gathered. As Sarah and Katie carried their trays in that direction, Sarah was trying to find Melanie's red head without appearing to do so. Melanie had hardly spoken to her since that first day. At recess, she spent the time with Martha Waterhouse and Wanda Wiggins. The three of them walked around, talking and laughing, with their arms around each other's waists. Sarah didn't exactly care, but she did wonder what they were talking about.

"I've been in lots of plays," Melanie was saying

carelessly as Sarah and Katie found places at the end of her table. "At home, I took acting lessons, and we did a different play every month."

"And you're going to be in our play, aren't you?" Martha Waterhouse said, with a sidelong glance at Sarah.

Melanie laughed. "If I can choose my part," she said.

"Of course you can choose," Wanda Wiggins said, her round face shiny and earnest. "You can have any part you want."

Melanie's eyes danced at Sarah and Katie. "You might not win," she teased Wanda.

"Oh yes, we will," Martha said, and leaned across the table to whisper in Melanie's ear. Sarah was dying to know what she said, and she couldn't understand how Katie could go right on eating. *Will Melanie be in our play if we win?* she wondered. She went over the parts in her mind. There was a mother, and the poor children, but somehow Melanie didn't seem exactly right for them. Then a picture flashed into Sarah's mind. She saw a sick girl in bed. The girl had a pale, delicate face, and her red hair fanned out over a lacy pillow.

Oh, no, Sarah thought, horrified at herself. Katie was going to be Collette. They had decided that at the very beginning. But her eyes lingered on

Melanie's face, and when Melanie left with Wanda and Martha, Sarah sighed.

"Would you let Melanie choose her part in our play?" Katie asked.

Sarah squirmed. It was exactly as if Katie had read her mind.

"I don't know," she said carelessly. "We haven't won yet. Maybe Martha and Wanda have won."

Katie continued to stare at Sarah, and there was something so sad in her eyes that Sarah almost hoped they *wouldn't* win.

It was the longest afternoon Sarah had ever spent in school, but at last the clock ticked to two-thirty, and Miss Mulkey said, "Stand." Everyone rushed for the door. "Take your seats," Miss Mulkey snapped. "That is *not* the way we behave in school." Eddie Barker stuck out his tongue behind his cupped hand, and they hurried back to their seats to stand, and form lines, and march out in proper order.

Even with Miss Mulkey watching, however, it was impossible not to rush and whisper. Sarah and Katie hurried as fast as the rest, holding hands tightly the whole way. "In a minute, we'll *know*," Sarah whispered, and Katie nodded, her eyes round.

The first thing Sarah saw in the auditorium was

the untidy pile of papers on Miss Lane's desk. She nudged Katie, and Katie nodded. Their play was clearly visible near the top.

Miss Lane was writing as they came in. She gave them a vague smile, and went on writing for what seemed a long time. At last, she put the pink paper in her desk and stood up.

"I read your little plays last night, and I'm afraid most of them are too short," Miss Lane said regretfully. "A play has to be at least ten pages, or it will be over before it starts." Someone behind Sarah muttered, "She might have told us that before," and Katie squeezed Sarah's hand. Their play was sixteen pages long.

"The best three—" Miss Lane stopped for a long, agonizing minute to search the cluttered surface of her desk until she found a scrap of paper. "The best three were written by Martha Waterhouse and Wanda Wiggins—" There was a squeal from the end of the row. "—by Jim Hook and Glenn Anderson—" Someone gave a subdued cheer, and Miss Lane smiled. "—and by Sarah Abbott and Katherine Donnelly." Sarah felt herself almost rise out of her seat. Only Katie's hand kept her down. They were *one* of the best. "We will use the one that says the most about Thanksgiving." Miss Lane paused as if she were enjoying the suspense. "So the play I have chosen is *Thanksgiving for Collette* by Sarah and Katherine."

"Oh!" Sarah said out loud. "Oh, my."

Miss Lane laughed, Katie bounced in her seat, and Betty Evans leaned over to hug them both. Then Melanie, smiling delightfully, stood up and began to clap. The whole class clapped with her except for Martha Waterhouse, who ducked her head as if she wanted to cry.

"We won," Katie whispered. Her blue eyes beamed, and her cheeks were pinker than ever. "Oh, Sarah, we won!"

Then Miss Lane made it even better by announcing that the production would be entirely in the hands of the authors, and that until Thanksgiving the entire cast would use Auditorium period to practice in the office behind the stage.

Everyone, of course, begged to be in the play. Katie laughed with the excitement of it all, and Sarah, seeing her, was suddenly not quite so happy. Katie looked terribly healthy.

When the bell rang, Melanie jumped up and leaned over the back of her seat to catch Sarah's hand. "I'll be in your play," she said softly, "if I can choose any part I like."

3 / Sarah Abbott, Director

After school, Sarah and Katie ran all the way to Sarah's house to be hugged and kissed by Sarah's mother. Next, they streaked around the corner and up Alameda Drive to be hugged and kissed by Katie's mother. Then, while Mrs. Donnelly ironed and the Donnelly twins clung to either side of Sarah's chair, Sarah held the fat Donnelly baby and told the whole exciting story of the afternoon. When Katie had finished her chores and changed her dress, the girls ran all the way back to Sarah's house.

There, they found the dining-room table set with Mrs. Abbott's best lace cloth and good dishes. There were candles and flowers and even place cards. "For *us?*" Katie asked, and was so over-whelmed by the grandeur of it all that she didn't go to the bedroom while Sarah changed, but sat on the edge of a living-room chair, staring straight ahead like real company.

The celebration dinner was a grand success, and a thoroughly dressed-up occasion. Katie wore her Sunday pongee, Sarah put on her pink dotted swiss, and Mrs. Abbott was in the brown chiffon Sarah loved. Mr. Abbott was the most elegant of all in a green velvet smoking jacket. "I've never seen that before," Sarah exclaimed.

"I've never before found an event worthy of its magnificence," Mr. Abbott said, and Sarah nodded. This *was* an important event.

Toasts were proposed and speeches given, one by Mr. Abbott and one by Sarah. Katie blushed and shook her head when she was asked to speak, and Mrs. Abbott said Mr. Abbott might as well speak for both of them, since he was used to it. Sarah's speech was excellent, her mother said, but Mr. Abbott was so funny and sounded so serious as he talked of the "new American playwrights, Katherine Diane Donnelly and Sarah Jane Ab-bott," that Katie giggled and giggled, and could scarcely eat.

"This is so wonderful I can't believe it's me,"

31

she sighed as she spooned up the last of her ice cream and chocolate sauce.

"Lady Luck has smiled her enigmatic smile," Mr. Abbott said gravely, but Mrs. Abbott shook her head at him.

"Now, Tom, Lady Luck hasn't smiled any kind of smile at all. The girls have worked hard for their success and they deserve it."

"There's a lot more work," Sarah said. "We have to copy out all the parts, and we have to decide who's going to be in it, and then we have to practice and practice. Did I tell you, Daddy, that I'm going to be the director?"

"That's very brave of you," Mr. Abbott said, with the solemn look that told Sarah he was teasing.

"Why is it brave of me?" she asked, giggling.

"Because if the play is a success, everyone will praise the actors. If it isn't a success, they'll blame the director. Either way, you won't get any credit."

"I don't care," Sarah said contentedly. "I just want the play to be *good*."

Katie had been staring at the tablecloth and turning her spoon over and over. Now she looked up, scared but determined.

"Sarah," she said. "I've been thinking about—

about Melanie. She's been in all those plays in California, and the only time I've acted in my whole life was when I was a carrot in our health play in the second grade. So if you want"—her face grew pink and her voice faltered—"if you want Melanie to be Collette, it's all right. I can be somebody else."

Oh, dear, Sarah thought. Her face grew hot and she couldn't look at Katie. She *did* want Melanie to play Collette—Melanie looked so exactly right —but she didn't want to hurt Katie's feelings. She cast an imploring look at her father, but he was staring at the candles. *It's a terribly important thing to decide,* she thought.

"I—I think that's up to you, Katie," she said unhappily.

"No, it isn't." Mr. Abbott spoke quickly. "The director makes the decisions, Sarah. Right or wrong, she makes them." Sarah stared at Katie. And sighed. Katie could *never* look sick. She thought of Melanie's cool, pale face.

"I guess," she said slowly, "that Melanie does *look* more like a sick girl." Katie began to blink, hard.

"I think so, too," she said. "It's all right, Sarah." She sounded as if she meant it. Nevertheless, Sarah

34

felt as if she had slapped her best friend.

During the weekend, the girls made copies of the play and tried to decide who would be best for the various parts. On Monday they were surrounded by would-be actors the moment they reached the playground. Melanie walked directly toward them with a gay, friendly smile. "Hello, there," she called. She was wearing a gray coat trimmed with white fur and a white fur muff, and Sarah thought she was beautiful.

"Are you going to let me be in your play?" Melanie demanded. Katie looked at Sarah and Sarah nodded. "Can I play any part I like?" Again Sarah nodded, but doubtfully. What if Melanie didn't want to be Collette?

"Who has the most to say?" Melanie asked.

"Collette does," Sarah said.

Melanie tossed back her red hair, and smiled a slow, satisfied smile. "Then I want to be Collette." Sarah sighed with relief, but Melanie laughed. "What's the matter, Katie?" she asked. "Don't you think I can act?"

Katie was staring at Melanie without any expression at all. "Oh, yes," she said. "Yes, I think you can act."

The next moment, Melanie linked her arm

through Sarah's, smiling as if they were best friends. "You can carry my muff if you want to," she said.

Dazed with happiness at being singled out, Sarah walked up the steps with Melanie past Danny Wade, who stared at them, frowning, past Eddie Barker, who called, "Hey, Sarah—I can walk on my hands," and past tiny Mary Weston, who asked, "Are there any fairies in your play, Sarah?"

She was aware of Katie trailing behind, and it made her impatient. Why did Katie have to act so left out? Why couldn't all three of them be friends? At the same time, she remembered uncomfortably that it was *her* arm Melanie had taken, and it was into *her* hands the muff had been thrust. She turned her head to smile at Katie, and found herself staring into the hurt, indignant eyes of Wanda and Martha. Melanie had swept past them without a word or a look.

"Wait a minute," she said to Melanie, and ran to the two girls. "Katie and I want you both to be in our play," she said. "Will you?" Martha and Wanda exchanged glances. Then Wanda lifted her chin.

"*I* want to."

"So do I," Martha echoed.

As Sarah ran back to Melanie, she gave Katie's arm a quick squeeze. "Wanda's going to be perfect for the mother," she whispered. "She's so nice and fat."

Sarah was supremely happy that day. Everyone was nice to her. Eddie didn't tease, and Will Stevens gave her a piece of gum. Everywhere she looked, she saw friendly faces and warm smiles. All day, she planned the play in her mind. It was lovely to be a director.

"What if Miss Lane won't let you direct?" Katie asked at recess.

"She said it was entirely in our hands."

"Yes, I know." Katie nodded. "But that was last week."

"Oh, Katie," Sarah exclaimed impatiently, "if it was mean old Miss Mulkey, you'd believe her."

"Of course I would," Katie said, looking surprised.

Miss Lane, however, agreed readily that Sarah could direct. "It's your little play," she said, smiling gaily at Sarah. "I promise not to interfere."

Sarah felt a sudden alarm. "But you'll help, won't you?"

Miss Lane laughed. "That's my job, I'm afraid."

It seemed an odd way of putting it, but Sarah

forgot her momentary puzzlement in the excitement of announcing the cast. It was such fun to read the list of names and see the quick, delighted smiles. Melanie was Collette, of course, and Wanda Wiggins her mother. Will Stevens was the doctor, because he was tall. Martha Waterhouse, Betty Evans, June Tamanito, Mary Weston, and Melvin Peterson were to be children, and they had been chosen because they were short. Katie, who wasn't quite so short, was to be the oldest child.

When she had finished, Sarah saw so many disappointed faces that she added a name that wasn't on the list at all. "And Eddie Barker will be the bad boy," she said. The class laughed— Eddie was always in trouble—and Sarah was laughing, too, as she sat down.

"*What* bad boy?" Katie whispered to Sarah.

"It'll be all right," Sarah answered. "He doesn't have to say anything."

Sarah was glad she had included Eddie when they reached Miss Lane's office for their first rehearsal. It wasn't as easy to give orders as she had thought it would be, and Wanda, especially, was inclined to argue. "Why don't you shut up?" Eddie said to Wanda. "Sarah's the director. Let her direct."

Wanda made a face, but she was quiet after that, and listened as Sarah explained the parts. "The mother is worried and fusses a lot. The doctor is old, Will, and very dignified. Collette is rich, but the children outside are poor. That's why they don't have any warm clothes and are cold all the time. Collette feels terrible," she told Melanie. "She's sick and has to stay in bed, and they won't let her do *anything*."

When Melanie read the first line, "Mama, I'm thirsty," Sarah's heart leaped. Melanie was going to be good. She *sounded* tired and cross and thirsty.

The others weren't so good. Wanda rattled, Will mumbled, and even Katie sounded as if she were reading history. Sarah made suggestions, and they tried it again with so much more naturalness and feeling that Sarah was elated. It was fun being a director.

"You were awfully good, Sarah," Katie said as they walked toward their lockers. "You weren't scared a bit, were you? I would have been."

"I *was* scared," Sarah said. "I don't know what I'd have done if Eddie hadn't said what he did."

"I know. Wanda thinks she's so smart, but I think she's silly. I would have said something my-self, but I knew she wouldn't pay any attention to me." They walked in silence until they rounded the corner, and then Katie said, "I thought Melanie was good. She really can act, can't she?"

Sarah gave Katie a quick little glance. Her chin was up, and she was staring straight ahead. *Katie is so nice,* Sarah thought. She made her voice sound careless. "Sure, she's good, but she's had all those acting lessons, remember?"

"Sarah!" a voice called. It was Melanie, sliding down the hall toward them, her hair bouncing and her face alight. "Sarah, I just had the most marvelous idea," she said breathlessly. "Why don't we have some extra rehearsals after school? There's only five weeks left, you know, and that's really not enough." Her words rushed out. "You could come to my house. My mother wouldn't mind, and we could use the couch for a bed, you know, and it would seem more real."

The idea struck Sarah instantly as a good one. "Oh, yes, let's," she cried. It would be fun to rehearse after school, and she was dying to see Melanie's house. She imagined it would be grand and beautiful like the houses in movies.

"Let's do it tomorrow!"

Sarah came back to earth. "That's too soon. Everyone's gone now. They have to ask at home if they can come."

Melanie broke into laughter. "Do they have to ask their *mothers*? My mother lets me do anything I want." She lifted her shoulders in an amused shrug. "Oh, well. We'll do it Wednesday."

She ran away as quickly as she had come, and Sarah turned to Katie who was standing with her back against the lockers, looking stubborn. "I don't think I can," she said. "My mother doesn't know Melanie's mother."

"You aren't going there to *play*," Sarah said. "This is different. It's a rehearsal. You can ask her, can't you?"

Katie looked right into Sarah's eyes. "Do you want me to come?"

"Of course I want you to come," Sarah said. "It isn't any use rehearsing if everybody isn't there."

Katie smiled faintly. "All right, then. I'll ask."

Katie was waiting with the others at the side door of the school on Wednesday afternoon. Melanie had been kept in ten minutes for whispering. Eddie tried to walk the iron fence while they waited, and had just managed it when Melanie appeared, looking very pretty in her gray coat and black patent slippers.

"Here we go," she said gaily, and slipped her arm through Sarah's.

Up the hill they walked, and down Sandy Boulevard, all of them talking as fast as they could about the play, except Will Stevens, who kept saying that he hoped they knew he had to leave early for his paper route. When they came to the pretty cluster of brick apartments next to the firehouse, Melanie turned in. "Do you live *here*?" Sarah asked in surprise. She had never known anyone who lived in an apartment.

"Of course I do," Melanie laughed.

She ran ahead, pulling a key from her pocket, and Eddie said, "Golly," because none of them had ever carried a key. Melanie held the door open invitingly.

"Come on in, all of you," she said.

The room was large, and everything in it was blue or white. Sarah caught her breath. It *was* just like the movies. "Take off your coats," Melanie cried, and threw her own on a chair. Her dress matched the room exactly. Sarah smoothed her own crumpled skirt, and wondered if she could talk her mother into letting her wear her dotted swiss the next day. "I made some lemonade," Melanie said, and disappeared around a corner.

They all stood where they were, staring at each other uncertainly. *We look like the beggar chil-*

dren in the palace, Sarah suddenly thought, noticing June's scratched knees and Eddie's hanging shirttail. Then Katie tugged at her arm.

"It's so still," she whispered. "I wonder where her mother is?"

It *was* still. The room had a planned look, like a furniture store, and there wasn't any friendly clutter around; no books or magazines or pieces of knitting. It was almost as if no one lived there.

"Here we are," Melanie called gaily, and came in bearing a large tray loaded with glasses, a tall pitcher and a plate of store cookies. She placed the tray on a low table. "Everyone help themselves."

It was like a party. They filled their glasses and then sat on the edges of their chairs, sipping politely. Eddie was the only one who had the courage to take more than one cookie. Melanie danced about, laughing excitedly and urging them to have more of everything. Suddenly, she twirled the piano stool, sat down and crashed both hands against the keyboard. At the sudden noise they all jumped, and Martha gave a little shriek.

"Ladies and gentlemen," Melanie announced in a deep voice. "I will now play for you my favorite song." She gave her red hair a toss and began to play. Her thin hands flew over the keyboard, and the music rollicked through the room.

"California, here I come!" Melanie sang in a high, sweet voice, smiling at them impishly over her shoulder.

"Right back where I started from . . ."

Sarah felt a thrill crawl up her backbone. How Melanie could play! Everyone kept time, Eddie pretended to conduct, and Will leaned forward with his mouth hanging open. When Melanie finished with two tremendous bass chords, Sarah found herself clapping wildly with the rest.

"Boy," Will said reverently. "You really can make the old keys dance. Can you play anything else?"

"Anything you want," Melanie laughed. "I play by ear." She began their school song, and first June and then Wanda joined in until all of them were singing. "Over There" followed the school song, and then "I've Been Working on the Railroad" and "Row, Row, Row." She played everything they knew, and Sarah was having so much fun she didn't realize how the time was passing until Will glanced at the clock on the mantel and jumped to his feet.

"I've got to go," he said abruptly, catching up his jacket. "Thanks for the lemonade." He slammed the door as he ran out, and the party-feeling ended as suddenly as it had begun. Every-one realized how late it was.

"Aren't we going to rehearse at all?" Katie asked. "I thought that was why we came."

"Yes, we are," Sarah said. She jumped to her feet and began to give directions very fast to make up for the time they'd lost. "We'll pretend that's the window, and this chair is the door, and the couch is the bed. Come on, Melanie, let's start."

It wasn't a satisfactory rehearsal. Sarah read Will's part, but it wasn't the same as having him there. And Melanie wouldn't be serious. She flopped about on the couch, groaning loudly and clutching her head and stomach. Wanda giggled, and Sarah told them both to stop it.

"Am I doing something wrong?" Melanie asked with pretended innocence. "She's supposed to be sick, isn't she?"

"Not groaning sick," Sarah said.

"All right. I won't groan." But she writhed and made such terrible faces that even Sarah had to laugh. And then the clock on the mantel chimed.

"Five o'clock!" Katie said. "I have to go home."

"Five o'clock!" Melanie jumped up and raced out of the room. Sarah looked at Katie. It seemed odd that she wouldn't even wait to say good-bye. Silently, they put on their coats and jackets. June

45

had just opened the door when Melanie came back, wearing a kimono and bedroom slippers. Her hair was tied with a ribbon and she looked different, more subdued.

"We'll do it again tomorrow," she said, and Sarah had the impression that she was rushing them out. As they walked past the window, she caught a glimpse of Melanie, frantically gathering up the empty glasses. It was all very odd.

"That wasn't much of a rehearsal," Katie said when they were alone. Eddie and Melvin lived down the hill by the school, and June, Mary, Wanda, and Martha lived across Sandy Boulevard.

Sarah sighed. "No, it wasn't, and it was my fault. I should have made them start sooner."

"It wasn't your fault at all," Katie said loudly. Her eyes flashed, and her mouth was angry. "It was Melanie's fault. She didn't want to rehearse. She only wanted to have fun." Her feet slapped at the pavement. "I'm not going again. It's a waste of time. Anyway, my mother won't let me go if Melanie's mother isn't home."

"Maybe she will be there tomorrow," Sarah said.

"I don't think so. *I* think her mother works. And I don't think she knows Melanie wears her best clothes to school, either. Did you see how quickly

she ran and changed when it was five o'clock?"
Sarah had noticed, but she didn't like Katie pointing it out to her.

"Lots of people are supposed to change after
school," she said.

"Into play clothes. Not a bathrobe."

"What's the difference?"

"A lot of difference."

Katie was shouting, and Sarah shouted right
back. "You don't like Melanie. You never have. *I*
think you're jealous!"

"Oh!" Katie looked as if she were so angry she
could hardly speak. She planted herself on the
sidewalk and thrust her fists against her hips.
"Well, if that's what you think, Sarah Abbott, you
can just go ahead and think it. *I* don't care."

She began to run, jerkily, as if she were crying.
Her yellow braids bobbed. Sarah watched her go,
through a mist of angry tears. *Let her go,* she
thought. *She's jealous. Just because I'm friends
with Melanie. Well, I don't care. Melanie is my
friend, and if Katie doesn't like it* . . . She trailed
home through fallen leaves, feeling bitterly unhappy and misunderstood.

When she reached home, the kitchen was full of
dinner smells, and her mother was at the stove,

stirring gravy. "You're late, Sarah," she said. "I didn't expect you to be this late."

"I'm sorry."

"I think you should plan to be home by five after this."

"All right." Sarah went to the back hall to hang up her coat, and to avoid her mother's searching look.

"Was it a good rehearsal?" Mrs. Abbott asked, bending to look in the oven.

"It was all right, I guess."

"Tell me about Melanie's house. Is her mother nice?"

Sarah turned her back. Her face grew hot, and her stomach hollow. She wanted to tell all about Melanie's house, and that her mother wasn't there and that they didn't rehearse, and about her quarrel with Katie. She wanted to feel her mother's comforting arms and hear her warm voice saying it would be all right. But she didn't dare. If she told, she would never be allowed to go to Melanie's again. She couldn't let the others go without her. She was the director.

"I guess so," she said. "Shall I set the table?" And she ran into the dining room to hide her flaming face in the tablecloth drawer.

4 / The Diamond Ring

There was no friendly tap from Katie on Sarah's door the next morning, and Sarah walked to school alone. The sky was misty, and the wind blew wet drops from the trees and bushes as if the whole world were crying. When she reached the playground, Katie was jumping rope with June Tamanito. Sarah stared a long time in their direction, but Katie didn't seem to see her.

At home in bed the night before, when she was still pretty mad, Sarah had thought she would positively enjoy walking home with Melanie right in front of Katie. But when Melanie was finally ready to leave that afternoon, Katie was nowhere in sight.

It was a smaller and more silent group that followed Sarah and Melanie up the hill, past the firehouse, and into the pretty brick apartments. Katie wasn't the only one missing. Betty Evans hadn't come, or Melvin Peterson. Will Stevens stayed long enough to gulp down some milk and a good third of the cookies, and then said he had to go.

"There aren't enough of us to rehearse," Melanie said carelessly. "Let's sing."

Melanie's playing was as delightful as before, but somehow singing wasn't much fun. Sarah kept watching the clock and thinking that she ought to insist on a rehearsal, but she didn't know how to do it. She wasn't comfortable in this strange, empty-feeling room, and the absence of Melanie's mother seemed even more glaring than it had the day before.

When Eddie Barker left, all hopes of a rehearsal had to be abandoned. "Gotta see a man about a mouse," he said, and walked on his hands to the door. His shoelaces waved in the air, and Melanie laughed and applauded, but Wanda said, "He's showing off. He's always showing off."

Making a horrible face at Wanda that made Melanie laugh even harder, Eddie tipped himself upright, said, "Thanks for the stuff," and walked out, grinning.

A moment later, he walked right back in. "Guess who's out there," he said, going to the window. "Come here."

The girls crowded around him, peering through the blue curtains. Sarah couldn't see anything at first except the lawn and bushes in front of the apartments. Then Wanda whispered, "What's he doing here?" When Sarah followed her pointing finger to the sidewalk, she saw a boy—a big boy in a ragged jacket—leaning against a telephone pole. As they watched, he turned his head toward the window. Sarah stepped back with a panicky feeling inside her. It was Danny Wade.

"He's watching us," Martha said in a frightened whisper.

Melanie tossed her hair and shrugged. "It's a public sidewalk. I guess he can be there if he wants to."

"But what if he stays until we have to go home?" Martha wailed.

Melanie regarded her with amused eyes. "Are you afraid of him?"

"Yes," Martha said.

"Are you?" Melanie asked Eddie.

"Oh, no, no. Not at all." Eddie rolled his eyes until the whites showed, and knocked his knees together in mock terror. "I'm not a bit s-s-scared of him, but if you've got a back door, I'll use it."

Everyone laughed except Melanie, who said with a scornful curl of her lip, "You'll have to go through the basement. The door's at the end of the hall."

"I'll remember you in my will," Eddie said fervently, and dashed out.

"What a lot of scaredy-cats!" Melanie flicked the blue curtains together. "He's not going to eat you."

"It's all very well for you to talk, Melanie Rivers," Martha cried. "You don't have to walk home."

"I wonder what he's doing here?" Mary Weston said thoughtfully. "He lives way down on Klickitat."

"Maybe he followed us." There was malice in Martha's voice. "Maybe he likes Melanie."

Melanie went scarlet. She swung around to face Martha with her hand upraised as if she were going to slap her. Sarah gasped, June's dark eyes grew round. Melanie looked from one horrified face to the other, and let her hand drop. "Let's do something," she exclaimed. "This is stupid. Let's call people up."

"Call who?" Wanda asked.

"Oh, anybody. Haven't you ever done that? Here, I'll show you." She darted to the phone table and caught up the telephone book. "Put your finger on it," she said to Sarah, opening the book at random.

Sarah did as she was told. Melanie peered at the spot, giggled, and dialed. When she spoke, her voice was serious and much older.

"Are you the lady who washes?" she asked, and held the receiver so the girls could hear, too.

"I most certainly am not!" a woman's voice said indignantly.

"You don't wash? Oh, you dirty thing!" Melanie hung up in a burst of laughter.

Sarah laughed with the rest, but she was uncomfortable. She knew what her mother would think of such a call.

"Do it again, Melanie," Wanda said eagerly.

Melanie did do it again. She did it several times, but after a while the game palled, and they wandered away from the telephone.

"I have an idea," Melanie cried. "Now, don't look." She held the telephone book so they couldn't see, and ran her finger down the columns. When she had found what she wanted, she made a mischievous face at them, and dialed. She asked her question, but before the girls could hear the answer, Melanie gave a shriek of laughter and slammed the receiver onto the hook. She laughed so hard that the tears ran down her cheeks, and Sarah became alarmed.

"Are you all right?" she asked. "What's the matter, Melanie?"

"It was Danny Wade's mother," Melanie gasped, "and when I asked, 'Are—are you the lady who washes?' she said—" She shrieked again. "She said —'Yes!' "

Martha and Wanda screamed with Melanie, but no one else laughed.

"I don't think that's very funny," June Tamanito said stiffly, "and I'm sorry, Melanie, but I must go home now."

"What time is it?" Sarah gasped. She had completely forgotten to watch the clock.

"Almost five," June said, "and I promised my mother—"

"I have to go, too." Sarah caught up her coat. "Good-bye, Melanie. See you tomorrow."

"What's the rush?" Melanie asked, still smiling over her joke. "I'll bet you're mad because we didn't rehearse. Never mind. Next time you can direct all you want to."

Sarah opened her mouth indignantly, and then closed it. There wasn't time to argue. As she dashed out the door, however, Melanie's bright, amused look stayed with her, and Sarah felt hurt. She had thought Melanie really liked her.

It wasn't until she passed the firehouse that she remembered Danny Wade. Her heart gave a thump, and she glanced quickly behind her. The sky in the west was murky red, and blue dusk had fallen over the street. Across Sandy Boulevard the lights of the drugstore spilled out over the sidewalk. The yellow square of a streetcar clanged past. There wasn't a boy in sight.

Still, Sarah began to run. She knew she was late, and besides, she had the breath-catching sense that Danny was there, someplace. Breathing hard, she pounded past the vacant lot and the dark, silent church. She was almost to the corner. After she turned it, there was only one house to pass, and she would be home.

Just as she reached the big snowball bush on the corner, a dark figure moved out of the darker shadow behind it. The streetlight fell on his face. It was Danny. His shoulders were hunched under his thin jacket and he glowered at her. Sarah came to an abrupt halt, her knees limp.

"You been down there?" Danny asked in a surly voice, jerking his head in the direction from which Sarah had come. Sarah swallowed twice and then nodded. Her voice seemed lost.

"What're you doing down there?" Danny said.

"Rehearsing," Sarah said in a small voice.

"Didn't look like rehearsing to me."

"Not all the time," Sarah said desperately. "Not every minute."

"Huh." Danny considered her, and then his lips parted in an unpleasant grin. "You think you're pretty smart, don't you?"

Sarah shook her head.

"Plays are dumb," Danny said loudly. "You're all dumb. I wouldn't be in your dumb old play."

Sarah was too frightened to speak. Danny didn't move. He stood in her path, his big fists against his hips, staring down at her, while Sarah stared back. For a moment—only a moment—she thought she saw something bewildered and hurt in his eyes. Then his hand flew out and gave her a shove, and he ran across the street, his feet flying out to the sides.

It wasn't a hard shove, and Sarah wasn't hurt, but she was shaking. Danny had disappeared. The dusky street was empty. Gradually, Sarah's fear subsided into a quivering excitement. She could hardly wait to tell the others! Wouldn't Katie stare? Then, abruptly, she remembered that Katie wasn't speaking to her.

Feeling more lonely than she had ever felt in her life, Sarah stumbled home.

*   *   *   *

It rained the next day, and the next, and all the following week. Low clouds raced across gray skies, and the wind blew cold rain into Sarah's face as she sloshed her way to school through puddles, and later, trailed Melanie home. The trees dripped monotonously, and the world was damp, chilly, and miserable.

Sarah was miserable. Katie acted as if she didn't exist, and linked arms with Betty Evans, looking perfectly happy. Once Sarah heard Betty say something that sounded as if she were spending a lot of time at Katie's house, and it made Sarah feel sad and empty. Every afternoon, she watched Katie run across the playground before she turned to go with Melanie to the apartment.

She didn't know why she went. She didn't enjoy herself, but still, she couldn't bear not to be there. Excitement sparked from Melanie. She showed Sarah and Wanda and Martha—the only ones who came, now—the contents of her mother's closets and drawers, and urged them to try on her mother's jewelry. They daubed themselves with lipstick and rouge. They made fudge without permission. There were more phone calls, and when they grew bored, Melanie brought out her snapshots and showed them the strange land she came from, where you could swim in the winter, and play under palm trees.

Sarah felt guilty about the things they did. She was sure Mrs. Rivers wouldn't like it, but since she had never seen Mrs. Rivers, the guilt was remote.

Every day they peeked out through the blue curtains to see if Danny Wade was waiting and watching. Once or twice they thought they saw him, and on those occasions Sarah ran all the way home with her heart jumping, but Danny never stopped her again.

She always left promptly at a quarter to five, not wanting to risk her mother's questions. One day, however, when they had made and eaten a pan of brownies, it took longer than they thought to tidy the kitchen, and it was almost five when they ran to the window to make sure Danny wasn't outside. Sarah had caught only a glimpse of a woman in a raincoat when Melanie jumped back and swished the curtains into place.

"It's my mother!" She looked around wildly. "You'll have to hide. Go in the kitchen. No! Go in my bedroom."

Sarah was astonished at Melanie's agitation. She was also dismayed. "I have to go," she said. "My mother—"

"Oh, blast your mother!" Melanie stamped her foot. "Will you hurry?" Wanda and Martha had already run across the blue carpet and disappeared into Melanie's bedroom.

"But Melanie—" Sarah protested.

Melanie's eyes blazed. She grabbed Sarah's arm, dragged her across the room, and almost flung her into the bedroom. Coming in, herself, she ripped off her blue velvet dress without a glance at the three girls, flung it on the floor of the closet and struggled into the kimono Sarah had seen before. She was kicking off her slippers, when the door of the apartment opened and closed, and a tired voice called, "Mellie? Mellie, where are you?"

"I'm in here, Mama," Melanie called calmly, although at that very minute she was feverishly tying back her hair with a black ribbon. "I'll be right out."

With a last, fierce look at Sarah, she slipped out,

leaving the door slightly ajar. Sarah moved to close it, but Wanda and Martha shook their heads so vehemently that she jerked her hand back from the knob as if it had been hot. Tiptoeing to the bed, she sat down, feeling worried and uncomfortable. She wasn't used to such deceptions, and she was going to be terribly late.

"You're early, Mama." Melanie's voice floated clearly through the apartment.

"I know. I got off a little early and I took a taxi. I couldn't face the streetcar after being on my feet all day." Mrs. Rivers' voice was high and pretty, but weary, as if every word were an effort. "You look nice and comfortable. Have you been reading?"

"I get tired of reading," Melanie said.

"Poor baby. You're lonesome, aren't you? Hand me my cigarettes, there's a darling." Sarah sat up. She had never known a mother who smoked. "I do wish you could make friends, honey. Isn't there some nice girl who would invite you to her house?"

"I don't want to go to anybody's house," Melanie said.

"Well, it's up to you," Mrs. Rivers said, but she sighed in a way that made Sarah suddenly feel sorry for her. "I wish you could try and like it here,

Mellie." There was no answer, and she sighed again. "Honey, I'm so tired. All I want is a hot bath and to lie down. Can you fix yourself some soup and toast? Oh, and here's some doughnuts I brought you."

"Thank you, Mama." Melanie's voice was even, and suddenly Sarah felt sorry for Melanie. Soup and toast for *dinner*! And no one to eat with.

"You'll be all right, won't you?" Mrs. Rivers asked, and added in an uncertain voice, "Don't you have homework or something?"

"Some," Melanie said.

"Well, get it done, and if I don't wake up be sure and go to bed on time."

"I will, Mama."

There was a silence. Martha, with an impish look, crept to the door and put her eye to the crack. Wanda followed. Then Mrs. Rivers spoke again. Her voice was much nearer and pleading.

"Mellie—darling—I'm doing the best I can. You know that, don't you?"

"Yes, Mama," Melanie said.

Sarah's eyes stung with tears. She jumped to her feet, and leaned over Wanda's bulky body, just in time to see Mrs. Rivers cross to her bedroom, her shoes in her hand. Sarah almost gasped.

Melanie's mother was young. She didn't look like a mother at all. Her red hair was short and curly, her green dress was tightly belted, and she wore bright lipstick. Sarah felt dazed. No wonder Melanie was pretty if her mother looked like that.

They were still crouched by the door when Melanie appeared with her finger on her lips. With an unfriendly look, she beckoned as if she wanted nothing so much as to be rid of them, and led the way to the front door. "I'm going to see if the paper's here, Mama," she called, and opened the door. As soon as the girls had slipped out, it closed behind them.

Wanda and Martha began to giggle almost immediately. Melanie was so clever, they said. Her mother hadn't suspected a thing. Sarah was too disturbed to answer. Besides, she was late. She ran all the way home, trying not to think of tired Mrs. Rivers, and of Melanie eating her lonely bowl of soup.

"You're late again, Sarah," her mother said. "You must be rehearsing very hard."

"I—I guess so," Sarah stammered, and gulped back tears. When she was in bed that night, she cried and cried for no reason at all.

After that, Sarah was more uncomfortable with

Melanie than ever. At recess, she was drawn into Melanie's tight, giggling little circle from which she cast longing looks at Katie and the others playing Red Rover or Giant Steps. Everyone thought that Sarah and Melanie were best friends, and it made Sarah feel odd, because in a way they were; but they never talked as she and Katie had, and she never knew what Melanie was thinking. Melanie, for instance, never made the slightest reference to the day the girls hid in the bedroom. It might not have happened.

The only bearable part of the day was Auditorium period, but even pretty Miss Lane had grown absentminded, and her smiles were not as warm as they had been. Still, she was better than Miss Mulkey, who picked on Sarah constantly. In the back of her mind, Sarah knew she was doing poor work, but Miss Mulkey's continual "Sarah, pay attention," "Sarah, I can't accept this paper," made her nervous and she made more mistakes than ever.

The rehearsals in the office back of the stage had grown dull and spiritless. Katie was always solidly there, and always did her best. Sarah was grateful, and would have liked to tell her so, but whenever she looked Katie's way, Katie looked at the floor. Sometimes, Sarah remembered how soon it would be Thanksgiving, and then she grew frightened, because Miss Lane hadn't said another word about helping. Sarah didn't see how she could manage the costumes and scenery alone, and she wished a dozen times that she could talk to Katie about it. After all, it was Katie's play, too. But Katie seemed to have forgotten that. Everyone was leaving everything to Sarah.

At this low point in Sarah's life, she wished every morning that something different would happen, but when something finally did happen, she wished it hadn't.

It was the second Monday in November, and school was topsy-turvy from the beginning. Sarah started late, and had to run the whole way, and then as she rushed up the stairs to the second floor, she saw Miss Lane ahead of her, all dressed up and carrying a small suitcase. Miss Lane must have just gotten back from a trip.

As Sarah scurried past, Miss Lane pulled open the big door of the auditorium, and Sarah caught a glimpse of her face. Her eyes were pink and swollen, as if she had been crying.

It shocked Sarah, and when she rounded the corner and found the whole sixth grade in the hall in coats and jackets, she felt as if the world were turning upside down.

"Keep your coat on, Sarah," Miss Mulkey said. "There will be a fire drill this morning." Sarah sighed with relief. Fire drills were normal.

When the drill was over, the entire school went to the auditorium to hear the fire chief talk, and they had no sooner returned to their room than Miss Mulkey sent Sarah on an errand to the office.

She dawdled on the way back, hoping to miss the spelling test, and when she reached the sixth-grade room, she waited quite a while in the hall before she slowly opened the door—and stood still in astonishment. The room was empty.

Sarah was angry. It was mean of Miss Mulkey to send her to the office without telling her it was nearly lunchtime! Hurriedly, she dragged her coat from the locker and pulled on her galoshes. Outside, the wet streets were deserted. Sarah was almost crying as she ran up the driveway and pulled at the back door. It stuck. She pulled again, and then she realized it was locked.

Panic-stricken, Sarah pounded as hard as she could. After a moment, quick footsteps sounded inside, and her mother opened the door.

"Why, Sarah," she exclaimed. "What are you doing home at this hour? Are you sick?"

"Isn't—isn't it lunchtime?" Sarah stammered.

"No, it isn't. It's over an hour until lunch. How

in the world did you get so mixed up. You'd better run back to school as quickly as you can and explain to Miss Mulkey."

Sarah stared. Go back and say she didn't know when lunchtime was? "I can't," she wailed. "Miss Mulkey is too mean."

"Nonsense," Mrs. Abbott said briskly. "Miss Mulkey is a very pleasant person, and I'm sure she will understand. Now trot."

There was nothing else to do. As she stepped off the back porch, rain blew in Sarah's face. She ran; it was too wet to walk. Her heart pounded as she crept upstairs to her locker, took off her wet things, and faced the closed door of the sixth-grade room. As she gulped for courage, the door opened and Miss Mulkey stepped out.

"Sarah, where have you been?" she asked sternly.

"I thought it was lunchtime," Sarah said, blinking back tears. She wouldn't cry in front of Miss Mulkey. Hard light glinted from Miss Mulkey's glasses, and her eyebrows rose. "There wasn't anyone here," Sarah said desperately.

Miss Mulkey's shoulders began to shake, and Sarah heard a soft sound almost like laughter as Miss Mulkey's hand touched her head.

"Good heavens, child, you're soaked," she said. "I'm terribly sorry. I should have told you to come to the gymnasium, but it's been such a hectic day, I didn't think." She bent down and put an arm around Sarah's shoulders, and for the first time, Sarah saw smiling gray eyes behind the bright glasses. "I *am* sorry, Sarah. Were you frightened?"

"I was scared to come back," Sarah admitted.

Miss Mulkey laughed out loud and squeezed her. "Well, there's no harm done, is there? Come in now, and let's see what we can learn before it really is time for lunch."

Sarah wrote her spelling words in an astonished daze. Miss Mulkey wasn't mean. Miss Mulkey liked her. It was almost too much for Sarah to grasp.

It was surprising what a difference it made. Her lessons seemed interesting again, now that she knew Miss Mulkey wasn't picking on her. When it was time for Auditorium that afternoon, Sarah looked at the clock in wonder. The day had passed so quickly.

As they entered the auditorium, Miss Lane, who always smiled so sweetly at them, frowned. Her mouth was set in a hard line. "Take your seats. Now!" she snapped at Eddie and Will, who were scuffling in the aisle. Eddie was so surprised that he blurted, "What's the matter with *her*," right out loud.

68

Miss Lane gave him a quelling look, and turned to Sarah. "Today," she said, "we'll see a rehearsal of your play."

Sarah's heart gave a bump. She glanced at the others and saw consternation on every face. If only Miss Lane had warned them!

"Well, you see—" she began, but Miss Lane interrupted icily.

"Don't tell me you haven't been rehearsing?"

"Yes, we have," Sarah said indignantly, "but—"

"Then we'll see how the play is coming. Go and get ready."

Slowly, the cast stood up and filed toward the backstage door. Miss Lane turned to the others. "While we are waiting, let's see how much you remember of Music Appreciation. If you recognize the name of the piece and the composer, write it on a slip of paper and hand it in at the end of class."

She put a record on the phonograph and then turned her back to the class, half sitting on the edge of her desk, her shoulders drooping. Her open purse stood beside her, and the drawer of the desk was pulled out.

As the lovely, sad strains of "Clair de Lune" floated through the room, Sarah stopped a moment

69

at the backstage door. She was sure it was by Debussy. Half the class must have known as well, because they scribbled eagerly. Miss Lane paid no attention. Her face, visible only to Sarah, was sad—as sad as the music—and her white hands twisted and untwisted in front of her red blouse. Then she drew a long, sighing breath and looked up. When she saw Sarah, her expression changed.

"Sarah," she said sharply over the music. "Didn't I tell you to get ready?"

"Yes, Miss Lane," Sarah gulped, and fled through the door and up the steps to the stage where the others were huddled, telling each other that they were sure they wouldn't remember a thing. Only Melanie and Wanda were at the front of the stage, peering out through the curtain.

"What's the matter with Miss Picklepuss?" Eddie whispered, making a face in the direction of the closed curtain.

"I don't know," Sarah said, "but we've got to get ready. Fix the chairs." She hurried to Wanda and Melanie.

"She's not wearing it now," Melanie was murmuring.

"Well, she had it on at fire drill," Wanda said importantly, "because I saw it."

"Let's get started," Sarah whispered to them, wondering what they were talking about.

It was a strange rehearsal. The stage was bigger than the tiny office, it was their first audience, and the whole cast seemed upset by Miss Lane's crossness. Will, who knew perfectly well what to do and say, stumbled over both his feet and his lines. Katie looked scared, and Wanda mumbled. Melanie, however, threw herself into her part with her usual abandon, and seemed to enjoy it. Sarah hid in the corner by the curtain to whisper Will's words when he forgot, and to beg them silently not to be so slow and dull.

"That wasn't good at all," Miss Lane said when they had finished. "If you expect to do this play at Thanksgiving, I'd suggest some good hard work. What have you done about scenery and costumes?"

Sarah was thunderstruck. "You said you'd help," she blurted.

"Now, Sarah, it's your responsibility. I told you that. Did you expect me to do it for you? If you need help, come and ask."

The minute the bell rang, the cast gathered around Sarah. The others pushed and jostled at the desk, handing in their sheets of paper.

"She *did* promise to help," Eddie said, loudly

enough for Miss Lane to hear if she were listening. "But we don't need her. We can do it ourselves."

"How can we?" Sarah whispered. "I don't know anything about scenery."

"I think my father would help us," June Tamanito said.

"And we can borrow things," said Betty Evans. "I know where I can get a dollhouse."

"I'll lend my French doll," Katie said. Sarah turned eagerly, but Katie was speaking to Betty Evans, not to her. "I could take care of the costumes, too," Katie went on, looking right at Betty. "Then Sarah wouldn't have to bother about that."

Sarah was bewildered. Katie was still mad at her. But Katie was going to help! It made Sarah suddenly feel so much better that she began to get ideas of her own.

"There's a lot of scenery stacked behind the stage," she said. "Let's ask if we can use it."

"Don't ask her," Will said, with a dark glance toward Miss Lane. "Ask Mr. Scott. He's the one who knows about it." The white-haired janitor was a favorite with everyone, and Sarah felt that if he helped them, their success was almost assured.

"All right, I will," she said. "I'll ask him right after school."

As she hurried to her locker, she felt happier than she had in a long time. After weeks of not caring much, she suddenly cared a great deal about the play. And so did the others. It made them friends in a very special and important way.

No one seemed to be hurrying into their wraps that day. The boys were talking about a paper drive, Sarah and Mary Weston were wondering where they could borrow a blue silk bedspread, and Katie and Betty Evans were discussing costumes. But most of the girls were clustered around Melanie, and Sarah suddenly realized that they were discussing the absence of Miss Lane's sparkling diamond.

"I think she took it off during lunch," a voice said.

"No, she didn't," Martha cried. "She had it on after that."

"Someone's going to be mad at her," Melanie said slyly, and a chorus of giggles arose.

As Sarah listened, she remembered Miss Lane's sad face and twisting hands, and wondered if it had anything to do with the ring.

Right then, she heard a clatter of high heels, and turned to see Miss Lane almost running down the hall. Her face was anxious, her purse was in her hand, and one brown curl had come loose to bounce against her cheek. Jerking open the door of the sixth-grade room, she called Miss Mulkey's name.

Miss Mulkey came to the door and looked over her glasses. "Yes, Miss Lane?" she said, and smiled. Miss Lane clutched Miss Mulkey's arm and said something Sarah couldn't hear. Miss Mulkey's smile died, and her face grew stern. "No one is to go home until I dismiss you," she said to the class. "I'll only keep you a moment." She drew Miss Lane into the room and closed the door.

"What's that all about?" Eddie Barker asked loudly, but no one answered. Sarah had a sinking sensation in the pit of her stomach. Something was terribly wrong, and it concerned them.

It wasn't long before the door opened again, and Miss Lane hurried down the hall, looking, Sarah thought, rather upset, as if Miss Mulkey had spoken sharply to her.

"Come in, children," Miss Mulkey said from the doorway. She didn't look cross, only tired.

In an uneasy silence, they filed in and took their places. It was strange to sit in class all bundled up for the outdoors. Miss Mulkey stood by her desk, and looked searchingly from one face to the other.

When her eyes reached Sarah, Sarah squirmed uneasily, feeling for no reason at all as if she had done something wrong. What had Miss Lane said? Was it something about the play?

"Children," Miss Mulkey said at last with a sigh, "Miss Lane has just told me something disturbing and sad. Her diamond ring is missing." There was a startled gasp from the class. "Miss Lane believes that someone in this class—" She paused, and then went on firmly, "—that someone in this class may have—taken it."

The room was hushed.

Taken? Sarah thought in bewilderment. Someone had taken Miss Lane's ring? Then the true word came crashing into her mind. *Stolen!* Miss Mulkey meant the ring was stolen. Someone in their class was a thief!

5 / Rich Man, Poor Man, Beggarman, "Thief"

"This is a serious matter, children," Miss Mulkey said. She looked and sounded so sorry that Sarah was sure she believed one of them was a thief. "I hope we will discover that Miss Lane is mistaken and the ring has merely been misplaced. But it doesn't look as if that is the case."

Eddie Barker waved his hand in the air. "What makes her think it was one of us?" he asked when Miss Mulkey nodded to him. "Why our class?"

"That's a reasonable question, Edwin." Miss Mulkey paused, and then said gravely, "You see, Miss Lane was wearing the ring until just before seventh period. At that time she took it off, and put it in her purse. The purse was on her desk. She tells me that at the end of class, all of you crowded around the desk to leave papers." She looked at them questioningly, and every head nodded.

Not all of us, Sarah thought.

"As soon as you left the auditorium, she looked for the ring, and it was—missing."

Sarah caught her breath with the rest. Then anyone could have taken the ring, anyone at all. There had been so much confusion in the auditorium at the end, and Miss Lane hadn't been anywhere near her desk. She tried to picture the scene in her mind, and she remembered that Miss Lane had been on the other side of the room, looking out the window. She felt a quiver of indignation. Why hadn't Miss Lane looked after her old ring? Why had she left it lying around like that?

Mary Weston received permission to speak. "Maybe it's still in her purse," she said earnestly. "My mother's always losing things down in the lining of hers."

Miss Mulkey shook her head, smiling faintly. "No, Mary," she said. "It isn't in the purse."

Sarah had a sudden vision of Miss Mulkey looking for herself; shaking the contents of the purse out on her desk. If she said the ring wasn't there, it wasn't.

"I'm going out in the hall now," Miss Mulkey said, with another sigh. "I want you to come out one at a time, beginning with Mary. I will ask each of you a question. When you have answered you may go home." She paused. "You are on your honor not to talk in the room."

The fifteen minutes that followed were the most frightening of Sarah's life. One by one, the children got up and left. Every face looked guilty. Some of the girls were crying. Sarah could feel her heart beating against her ribs. Her hands were clenched together on the desk. She had known most of the class all her life. She couldn't believe that one of them would steal, and yet she found herself watching stumbling feet, searching faces that were too red, or too pale, and wondering: *Is it him? Is it her?* When she saw that Katie's head was down on her arms, her heart seemed to stop before she realized how silly that was. Katie would *never* do such a thing.

When Danny Wade's turn came, he shuffled sullenly up the aisle. His jacket was mended in back, and his shaggy hair hung over his collar. He pushed the door open, and everyone in the room heard him shout, "I didn't *take* her old ring!" before it slammed shut.

Sarah caught her breath, and glanced across the aisle at Melanie. Melanie was smiling to herself. Her thin fingers turned her gold bracelet around and around her wrist.

She knows, Sarah thought, and then wondered numbly what Melanie knew and how she knew it. Had she seen something? Heard something? And if she had, would she tell Miss Mulkey?

She was still wondering when Melanie got up and walked composedly to the door, buttoning the fur collar of her coat. Sarah held her breath. It might be all over in a minute if Melanie told.

But Betty Evans followed Melanie, and Will Stevens followed Betty. Miss Mulkey didn't come back in the room, and Sarah began to doubt that Melanie really knew anything after all.

At last there was no one left but Sarah and Eddie and two others. Sarah scrambled to her feet and hurried to the door. Her knees felt limp, and her lips were so dry she had to lick them. In the hall she found Miss Mulkey, standing as straight as ever, but looking weary.

"Sarah," she asked, looking right into Sarah's eyes. "Do you know anything about Miss Lane's ring?"

Sarah shook her head. Her face was hot. Maybe

Miss Mulkey thought *she* had taken it!

"Did you hand in a paper at the end of class?"

Again, Sarah shook her head. "We rehearsed the play—for the class. We didn't do Music Appreciation." Then as Miss Mulkey continued to look at her, she added reluctantly, "But we weren't far from the desk. We were right at the front of the aisle."

"Thank you, Sarah. You may go."

Sarah was free to stumble down the steps and into the wet world outside. Although a light rain wet her face, she walked slowly across the playground. There was a hollow, guilty feeling inside her. She didn't know anything about Miss Lane's ring. But someone did. Someone had taken it. Someone she knew. Danny Wade's face flashed into her mind, but she pushed it away. Danny was mean and frightening, but he wouldn't steal. That was criminal.

"Hey, Sarah, wait up." Eddie Barker panted to her side, his wet hair shining gold around his cap. "That was some third degree, wasn't it? I thought she was going to shine a light in my eyes, and get out her rubber hose."

"Oh, Eddie!" Sarah couldn't help giggling.

"But no kidding," Eddie said, looking worried, "I think old Mulkey thinks I did it."

"That's silly. You were right in front of me the whole time. You couldn't have done it."

"Yeah, but old Monkey-Face doesn't know that." He glanced up at her. "Who do you think did it, Sarah?"

"I don't know," Sarah sighed. "I can't believe anyone in our class would steal."

"Ha! That's all you know. Anybody'll steal if they're poor enough. Look at that story Miss Mulkey read us about the guy who stole a loaf of bread, for gosh sakes!" He nodded wisely. "And you'd be plenty surprised if you knew who's getting Thanksgiving baskets in our class."

"Thanksgiving baskets!" Sarah exclaimed. "In *our* class?"

"Yep. I saw the list, and there's three of them. I'd tell you the names, only I promised my Mom I wouldn't."

"Then don't," Sarah said quickly. They had reached the iron fence and she leaned against it, staring at Eddie. "Are you sure? That's awful, isn't it? That's charity."

"Oh, I don't know," Eddie said. "I'd sure take one if someone offered it to me. There's going to be good stuff in those baskets. My Mom's making brownies. Anyway, I'll bet anything that one of those baskets is going to the guy who stole that ring. And I'll bet I can find out which one. Sherlock Holmes, that's me."

He whipped out an imaginary magnifying glass, and peered at Sarah's face until she laughed. "Hey, it's going to pour buckets," he said suddenly, glancing up at the sky. "See you tomorrow, Sarah."

He started off like a sprinter. Sarah looked up at the black cloud hovering directly overhead and began to run. When she was halfway up the block, the rain poured down on her head as if it had, indeed, come from a bucket, and she was drenched and shivering when she burst in the back door. The kitchen was warm and fragrant with the smell of freshly ironed clothes.

"Why, Sarah," her mother said, looking up from the ironing board. "Aren't you rehearsing today?"

Sarah's mouth dropped open. Her face flamed. She had forgotten all about Melanie! "N-no—not today," she stammered.

Mrs. Abbott put the iron down and looked at Sarah closely. "You're soaked," she said. "Where's your umbrella?"

"I guess I left it at school."

"You'd better run and change. I'll fix you something hot to drink."

Sarah changed her clothes with an uneasy feeling in the pit of her stomach. She was almost sure her mother was going to ask questions. She made the cup of hot chocolate her mother handed her last as long as possible. When the last swallow was gone, Mrs. Abbott sat down across the table from Sarah and folded her hands.

"Now, Sarah," she said, "I think it's time we had a talk."

Sarah wasn't sure how her mother managed it, but within ten minutes she knew all about the rehearsals that weren't rehearsals, and that Melanie's mother was never home. She knew about hiding in the bedroom, and about the quarrel with Katie, and Miss Lane's diamond ring, and the Thanksgiving baskets. The first words had to be pulled out of Sarah, but then it was such a relief that it all gushed out like water from a faucet.

"That's quite a load of worries for one girl," Mrs. Abbott said when Sarah finished. Her eyes were grave. "I'm not at all pleased with you, Sarah. You deceived me."

"I didn't mean to," Sarah muttered.

"Didn't you? You know the rules, and you know they don't include playing at houses where no adult is home."

She sounded disappointed and Sarah's eyes filled with tears. "I'm sorry. I don't know why I did it. I didn't like being there."

"I suppose it was exciting," Mrs. Abbott said slowly. "Melanie must be a fascinating little girl."

"Oh, she is!"

"Not like Katie," Mrs. Abbott suggested dryly.

Sarah's eyes fell, and a flush crept up her neck. "Melanie's different," she said, her voice faltering.

Mrs. Abbott sighed. "I've known a few Melanies myself," she said, "and they're fun to be with. It's good to have all kinds of friends, Sarah, but it isn't good to be led. You let Melanie lead you, and that was your mistake. You didn't stop to think whether or not you were doing things *you* thought were wrong."

Sarah remembered the phone calls, and rummaging in Mrs. Rivers' closet, and her face grew redder. "I suppose I ought to be punished," she said hesitantly.

"You have been." Sarah's eyes flew open and a faint smile crossed Mrs. Abbott's face. "I think you've found out that doing wrong things isn't much fun."

They talked until it was almost time to set the table, and with every word, Sarah felt lighter and

happier. Her mother had such a comforting way of putting things. It was Mrs. Abbott's opinion that Katie would be ready to make up soon if Sarah was, and that what Sarah had best do now was to concentrate on the play. She didn't think that Thanksgiving baskets were any disgrace when men who wanted to work couldn't get jobs, and she was quite sure that the matter of Miss Lane's ring could safely be left to Miss Mulkey and Mr. Tuttle.

It was exactly what Sarah wanted to hear. She hugged her mother, feeling warm and safe again. Even the rain pelting against the windows had a friendly sound, and when Sarah put down her book that night, and turned out the light, she felt as if all the bad times were over.

"Sarah, are you asleep?"

Mrs. Abbott came into Sarah's room, and sat on the foot of the bed. "I've been talking to Melanie's mother on the phone," she said.

Sarah was so startled that she sat straight up in bed. "But you don't know her."

Mrs. Abbott smiled. "I do now."

"You didn't—" Sarah clasped her hands in a pleading gesture. "You didn't tell on Melanie, did you? About her clothes and letting us come to her house?"

Mrs. Abbott was silent a long moment. "Darling," she said at last, "you have to understand that I feel as loyal toward mothers as you do toward your friends. I had to tell her."

"Mama, you didn't."

"Sarah, listen." Mrs. Abbott's voice was very firm. "Rules are meant to keep you safe. Supposing that while you girls were alone, the apartment caught fire, or someone burned herself badly while you were making fudge. Or suppose someone saw you, and tried to get in. Would you have known what to do?"

"I suppose not. But nothing *did* happen."

"And babies sometimes crawl across the street safely. But if you saw a baby in the street, wouldn't you tell its mother?"

Sarah sighed. She could see the force of her mother's argument, but she was absolutely certain Melanie wouldn't.

"I'm glad I did call," Mrs. Abbott went on, "because now I understand more about Melanie, and I want *you* to understand. She needs our help, Sarah. She didn't want to leave her friends and come to Portland, and I'm afraid she isn't behaving very well about it."

"Then why did they come?"

Mrs. Abbott hesitated. "Melanie's father and mother were—they didn't get along. I don't know why. At any rate, Melanie and her mother came to Portland. Melanie entered school and Mrs. Rivers went to work. But Melanie isn't happy."

"I don't think she's unhappy," Sarah said. "She's got the best part in the play, and she has lots of friends."

"*Does* she have friends?" Mrs. Abbott asked, and suddenly Sarah wasn't so sure. Everyone followed Melanie around, but that wasn't the same as being friends. "At any rate," her mother said briskly, "I think we can help Melanie to have a good time without breaking rules. I want you to invite her here, Sarah."

"I don't know if she'll come," Sarah said. "Melanie likes to—to do things her own way."

"At least you can ask her." Mrs. Abbott kissed Sarah's forehead. "Good night, darling."

When her mother had gone, Sarah snuggled into the covers again, but she felt wide awake. Outside her window the bare branches of the cherry tree tossed against the sky, while a small and lonely looking moon tried to peek through the clouds. *Is Melanie lonely?* Sarah wondered. *What must it be like to leave your home, and your school, and all your friends—and your father!* Sarah tried to imagine leaving her father, and her eyes filled with tears. *Poor Melanie. Poor, lonely Melanie.*

Sarah's throat ached with pity, but as she drifted off to sleep she saw in her mind a cool, secret little smile, and thin white fingers playing with a gold bracelet.

The next morning, Sarah walked to school cheerfully. The sun was shining. The light it gave was pale and watery, but still it was the sun. It burnished the streets to pewter, and every puddle on the playground reflected the sky. Sarah looked for Melanie's red head and gray coat, but couldn't see her anyplace. Making a wide circle around some boys who were playing dodge-ball, she ran up to Wanda, who leaned against the brick building chewing gum as fast as she could before the bell rang.

"Where's Melanie?" she asked.

Wanda shrugged. "I guess she hasn't come yet," she mumbled through the gum.

Melanie still wasn't there when they went to their lockers, and when Sarah took her place, the seat across the aisle was empty. Just as the tardy-bell rang, Melanie came flying in, and swished into her seat without a glance at anyone.

Sarah stared. Whatever had happened to Melanie? Her red hair hung in two braids, and she wore a brown cotton dress with a prim white collar. Sarah peeked at her feet, and saw stout oxfords. She didn't look like Melanie at all, but strangely enough, she was prettier than ever.

All morning Sarah tried to catch her eye, but Melanie kept her eyes on her books. When she was called to the blackboard, she marched to the front of the room, did her problem, and marched back. Her face was white and remote, and Sarah, remembering all she had learned, felt terribly sorry. When they went out for recess, she ran directly to Melanie.

"Hello," she said. Melanie turned her green eyes on Sarah without a flicker of friendliness. She simply looked. Sarah moved her feet uneasily. "Do you want to come to my house after school?" she asked.

"No," Melanie said, and walked away.

Sarah stepped back as if she'd been slapped. *She feels bad,* she told herself, but when she saw Melanie run to Wanda and Martha and throw an arm around each of them, she understood. Melanie thought Sarah had told on her. Well, she had in a way, but she hadn't meant to. She'd really told on herself. She couldn't help it if Melanie was all mixed up in it.

"Can I see your bracelet, Sarah?" little Mary Weston asked at her elbow.

Sarah looked down, puzzled. "I haven't got a bracelet."

"Oh, I thought you might." Mary seemed embarrassed. "Melanie's got one, and so have Martha and Wanda. They made them yesterday at Melanie's. Weren't you there?"

"No," Sarah said, and turned red.

Mary looked at her curiously. "Are you mad at Melanie?"

"I think she's mad at me," Sarah said.

"Oh." Mary smiled. "I wouldn't worry if I were you. Melanie gets mad pretty easy."

Sarah saw Melanie's bracelet a few minutes later when she went to wash the mud off her hands. It was lying on the shelf over the basin, and its bright blue beads were beautiful. She was tempted to try it on, but she hadn't touched it when Melanie appeared in the mirror, braids swinging.

"That's mine," Melanie said. She snatched the bracelet and was gone before Sarah could say a word.

Sarah sighed. Melanie was really mad, but Sarah

didn't mind as much as she thought she would. Only now, she didn't have any special friend. She stared at herself in the mirror as she dried her hands. *If I were as pretty as Melanie* . . .

Before she could finish the thought, Betty Evans pushed open the door and said, "Sarah, you'd better hurry. Listen, Sarah, my father says he can get us a lamp that looks just like sunlight. For outside the window, you know. Isn't that swell?"

Then Sarah remembered what her mother had said about concentrating on the play. That was exactly what she'd do. She'd make a list of everything they needed, and right after school she'd talk to Mr. Scott about the scenery. She'd make it the best play that was ever done at Roseland School.

Sarah, however, hadn't counted on Danny, who seemed to have a talent for trouble. That very afternoon as they were finishing geography and it was almost time for Auditorium, Miss Mulkey suddenly dropped her pointer on her desk and strode back to Danny.

"Daniel Wade," she said in an awful voice, "what does this mean?"

Danny hung his head and didn't answer, but Sarah could see a dark, red flush creeping up his cheek.

"Dan, I'm disappointed in you. I'll take that, please." Miss Mulkey held out her hand, and Danny reluctantly placed a jackknife in it. Sarah nearly fell out of her seat trying to see what Danny had been doing with a knife. "That's school property, Dan," Miss Mulkey went on in the same severe voice. "Now it will have to be replaced. Do you think you can pay for it?"

Danny's head hung lower, and he shook it slowly. Miss Mulkey's voice softened a little. "I think you had better see Mr. Scott right after school, Dan. Perhaps you can make some arrangement with him." She swung around quickly, and caught the class gaping. "All right, children. Eyes front."

The class obediently looked at the map, but Sarah noticed that the eyes of those nearest Danny's desk went first to Melanie, and there were smirks on those faces. She was consumed with curiosity.

It wasn't long before her curiosity was satisfied. As the cast of the play assembled in the office behind the stage, Will Stevens reached out and jerked one of Melanie's braids.

"Hey, Red," he said. "Who's your boyfriend?"

Melanie whirled on him furiously. Two bright spots burned in her cheeks, and her fists were clenched. "Nobody," she shouted. "Nobody in this stupid school."

Will backed out of range, grinning. "Yeah? Then how come Danny Wade carved your initials on his desk?"

The color died from Melanie's cheeks. She stared at Will as if he'd gone mad. Her face grew so pale it was frightening. "He didn't," she said in an incredulous whisper. "He wouldn't dare." Turning her back on all of them, she stared out the window. Katie frowned at Will, the others glanced at each other uncomfortably, and there was no more teasing.

Sarah found it hard, however, to bring their minds back to the play. "Sure. I guess so," Eddie said absently as she asked him if he could bring a ball for the children to play with. When she asked Will if he had any idea where he could borrow a doctor's bag, he didn't even hear her.

It was discouraging. And Melanie was at the bottom of it. Or was it Danny? Both of them, Sarah thought, caused trouble wherever they went. She couldn't even talk to Mr. Scott after school, because Danny would be there.

The next morning Sarah was at school early, determined to see Mr. Scott. She had no sooner stepped on the playground than three girls ran up to her with news that put Mr. Scott and the play right out of her head.

"Oh, Sarah, guess what we know," cried Mary Weston.

"You'll never guess in a million years," said Martha Waterhouse.

"It's awful," said Wanda Wiggins solemnly. "Really awful."

Sarah looked from one excited face to the other with a sinking sensation. Whatever they knew, she was almost sure it meant more trouble.

"It's Danny Wade," Mary Weston said.

"He took it," Martha said.

"That's right, Sarah." Wanda's eyes almost popped from her round face. "Danny Wade stole Miss Lane's diamond ring."

6 / A Bracelet and a Phone Call

No one seemed to know how the story got started, but before she reached the school steps, Sarah heard a dozen times that Danny had stolen Miss Lane's ring.

She believed it. If everyone said so, it had to be true. Still, she couldn't help remembering Eddie's remarks about the Thanksgiving baskets, and Melanie's phone call to Danny's mother, and the look in Danny's eyes the night he stopped her. It was those things that made her feel sorry and sad.

Miss Mulkey was truly cross that morning. She drilled them in spelling and mental arithmetic until Sarah's head buzzed from thinking so fast.

When recess came, Miss Mulkey suddenly announced that they would stay in the room for a few minutes and play a game called "Gossip."

A dozen children were lined up across the front of the room with June Tamanito at one end, and Melvin Peterson at the other. Miss Mulkey bent down and whispered something in June's ear. June whispered to the child next to her, and so on. As the words were passed along, the children broke into giggles. By the time the words reached Melvin Peterson, he was laughing so hard he could scarcely obey when Miss Mulkey asked him to tell what he heard.

"The tooth—" Melvin gasped, "the tooth ate Lucy."

The class laughed with him, and a dozen voices asked Miss Mulkey what she had really said to June. Miss Mulkey faced them with a frosty smile. "I said, 'The truth is elusive.' Now, children, you may play outside for the remainder of the recess."

"That's a pretty good game," Betty Evans said as they clattered downstairs, "but I don't know what elusive means, do you?"

"I'm not sure," Sarah said absently. "I think it means it isn't there."

"That doesn't make sense," Betty said.

97

It doesn't, Sarah thought, and it didn't make sense for Miss Mulkey to play games with them. She never had before. As she ran out on the playground, she suddenly thought she knew why Miss Mulkey had done it. She was telling them not to gossip. Sarah wondered if Miss Mulkey knew what everyone was saying about Danny Wade.

The game caught on, however, and all over the school yard groups of children were lined up whispering to each other. Sarah was waiting for a whisper to reach her, when she heard Melanie's voice behind her.

"It's gone!" Melanie said dramatically. "I had it on at my locker and now it's gone."

"Oh, Melanie," Wanda wailed. "Your lovely bracelet."

"Maybe you dropped it," said Martha. "It was pretty loose."

"Whoever found it didn't give it back," Melanie pointed out. "I think somebody kept it. Some thief."

"Pay attention, Sarah," Betty said, but before she could whisper in Sarah's ear, two boys raced toward them. Danny Wade was in front with a muddy ball clutched to his shirt, and his head turned over his shoulder. Sarah sidestepped just as Danny went sliding past her. There was a gasp and bump from behind, and Sarah whirled.

Danny and Melanie were sprawled in a puddle, Danny's outstretched hands still clutching the ball. Melanie lifted a mud-streaked face, and her green eyes flashed. "Ugly, hateful boy," she muttered.

Danny scrambled to his knees. His face was stricken. "Gee—" he gasped. The girls had crowded around Melanie to help her to her feet, and try to brush the mud from her clothes. Sarah was too stunned to move.

"Oh, your lovely coat," Martha mourned.

Danny got up slowly, looking helplessly at Melanie. Wanda faced him, so angry she stamped her foot. "Clumsy!" she said.

"He did it on purpose," Melanie said coldly.

Danny's face flamed. "Why didn't you get out of the way?" he muttered, and loped off across the playground without a backward glance.

Melanie paid no attention to her clothes. She stared after Danny with narrowed eyes. "He'll be sorry," she said in a tight voice. "Just you wait and see. He did it on purpose."

"He did not," someone said. Sarah turned to see Katie, her feet planted stubbornly, her face indignant. "It was an accident. Anyone could see that. He wasn't looking."

Melanie transferred her gaze to Katie, and

laughed mockingly. "Guess who Katie likes," she said.

"Oh!" Angrily, Katie ran off, and Martha and Wanda led Melanie toward the school.

Sarah stood where she was. Katie was right, of course. Danny hadn't done it on purpose. He hadn't looked where he was going either. But he was sorry. He'd almost said so. And then Melanie had to act so mean. To her amazement, Sarah found herself feeling sorry for Danny Wade.

Then Sarah saw something in the mud, and bent to pick it up. It was Melanie's blue bead bracelet. *She didn't lose it after all,* Sarah thought, as she ran to catch up with the girls. "Here's your bracelet," she said to Melanie. "You dropped it."

Melanie grabbed it without a glance at Sarah. "So *he's* the one who took it," she said to Wanda. "I might have known it."

Sarah was puzzled. The bracelet had been lying exactly where Melanie had fallen. She didn't see how Danny could have dropped it. It was almost as if Melanie wanted them to believe Danny was a thief.

It was lunchtime before Melanie and Martha appeared in the classroom. They had received permission to go to Melanie's house, so that she could change her muddy clothes. Melanie's hair hung loose again, and she wore her blue velvet dress. It seemed to put her in a better humor. She even smiled, rather mockingly, at Sarah as they walked to the basement lunchroom.

Sarah was eating at school that day, because her mother had a meeting, so she decided to find Mr. Scott before the lunch hour was over. The room babbled with talk about Danny Wade and Miss Lane's ring, and some older girls even asked Sarah to tell them what had happened on Monday. Sarah would have felt important, if she hadn't been so uncomfortably aware of Danny, hunched in a corner all alone, eating out of a paper sack. *How does everyone know he took the ring,* she wondered. No one could tell her that. Everyone had heard it from someone else.

Sarah ate hurriedly, and then ran to the furnace room farther along in the basement, where Mr. Scott had his workroom and his desk. She had been there once or twice to dry her wet feet, or to take Mr. Scott a note. When she peeked in, she saw a lunch box and a thermos bottle on the desk, but there was no Mr. Scott. As she hesitated, wondering if she should wait for him, she heard the sound of a hammer someplace overhead. Thinking that it was probably Mr. Scott's hammer, she ran out and up the stairs.

The children were forbidden to be in the main hall during lunch hour, but Sarah walked along briskly, following the sound. She thought that if she saw a teacher, she could explain, and it would probably be all right. When she found Mr. Scott, he was in the first-grade room, nailing an edge on a table under the window.

"Well, now, if it isn't Sarah Abbott," he said, looking up from his work. "What can I do for you, Sarah?"

Sarah smiled. Mr. Scott seemed to know the name of every child in the school. "What are you making?" she asked curiously.

"I'm making a sand table. It's to hold the Sahara desert, I'm told."

"Oh, what fun!" Sarah ran to look at the table, and found a cardboard box on the windowsill full of tiny palm trees and tents and camels. She examined it with delight.

"It's for the little ones," Mr. Scott said. "I'm thinking you're too grown up for such things."

"Yes." Sarah put the box back. "What I wanted to ask you was—you see, we're giving a play for the Thanksgiving program—" Mr. Scott nodded as if he knew all about it, put his head on one side, and drove a last nail. "But I don't know how to make the stage look right. Could you help us?"

Mr. Scott tucked his hammer in his belt and looked at Sarah with his white brows drawn together. "You have a teacher in that class?"

Sarah looked at the floor. "Yes. But she said it was my responsibility. I mean, she said she'd help, but—Will said you knew all about the scenery and—" She was floundering.

"Humph!" Mr. Scott said, but he patted Sarah's shoulder and smiled. "Then I guess we'll have to see what we can do. If you can stay a bit after school, I'll come up to the auditorium and we'll talk about what's needed."

"Oh, thank you!" Sarah cried. She clasped both her hands around his. "Thank you so much. You've taken a tremendous load off my mind."

Mr. Scott muttered something she didn't quite catch about people who put loads on children's minds, and then he twinkled at her kindly. "You'd better be running along now, Sarah Abbott, before you get caught."

Sarah was so eager to find the others and tell them the scenery problem was solved that she didn't bother going back through the basement, but hurried along the main hall, sliding a little on the polished floor. As she neared the main office, however, she glanced at it apprehensively and began to tiptoe. And then she heard voices.

"He didn't do it," a woman's voice said shrilly. "Not my Danny. He's not perfect—I'm not saying that—but he doesn't take things." Sarah flattened herself against the wall, afraid to move for fear she'd be heard.

A man's voice answered, low and quiet, and then someone began to cry. It wasn't Danny. It wasn't a child at all. It was the woman, Danny's mother, sobbing out loud. Sarah's feet seemed frozen to the floor. She wanted to leave, but she couldn't seem to move. The woman's voice rose, almost screaming, and it seemed to Sarah that she could feel the scream in her own throat.

"I tell you he didn't! Wouldn't I know if he had? Where is it now if he took it? Tell me that! Where is it now?"

Then Mr. Tuttle spoke loud enough for Sarah to hear the words clearly. "I'm not accusing Dan, Mrs. Wade. I told you that. But a child phoned and said he had taken it. Since he's been accused, I had to talk to you."

"Who?" Mrs. Wade demanded shrilly. "Who said he took it?"

"I told you. I don't know who," Mr. Tuttle said wearily. His voice dropped, and Sarah found herself straining to hear. "The child was too frightened to give her name. But she says she saw Dan take the ring. I can't ignore that, Mrs. Wade. Much as I would like to, I can't ignore that. Now, I know you've been having a hard time—"

"Oh, you don't know. You don't know," Mrs. Wade said. "And now this trouble." Her sobs began again. "I don't think it's right, Mr. Tuttle, indeed I don't. I don't think it's right to believe that child and not believe my Danny."

A sob broke from Sarah's throat, and she began to run. She didn't care if Mr. Tuttle caught her or not. She had only one thought in mind. She wanted to go home.

As she stumbled down the stairs to the outside door, her elbows were suddenly caught in a firm grasp. "Sarah," said a stern voice. "What has happened?"

Sarah looked up. Miss Mulkey's severe face gazed down at her. "Oh," Sarah wailed, throwing her arms around Miss Mulkey's thin waist, "she's crying. Danny's mother is crying. In the office."

"Come," Miss Mulkey said. She put an arm around Sarah's shoulders, and led her, still sobbing, up two flights of stairs to the sixth-grade

room. There she put Sarah in a chair by her desk, and pulled a clean handkerchief out of a drawer. "Blow your nose," she said. Sarah blew. "Now, what is this all about?"

Sarah told her, a little frightened now, especially since she had to admit she had been in the hall without permission. Miss Mulkey stood by the window looking out, and listened silently. "Well, Sarah," she said at last. "You've learned at least that eavesdroppers seldom hear anything pleasant."

Tears flooded Sarah's eyes again. "I knew I should have left," she said. "But I couldn't."

"So," Miss Mulkey said on a sigh, and stared at Sarah a long time. "I don't know any more about Miss Lane's ring than you do, Sarah, but I do know this. There is no proof that Dan took it, and until we have proof we cannot—we must not— believe it."

"But everyone says he did," Sarah cried.

"Everyone!" Miss Mulkey repeated with scorn in her voice. "You're old enough to know, Sarah, that what everyone says is often false." She paused. "Do you remember when we read the Constitution of the United States?" Sarah nodded. "The Constitution is the highest law of the land, and it says that a person is innocent—absolutely innocent—

107

until he is *proved* guilty. That means, Sarah, that we cannot give way to gossip, or even to our own suspicions. We must believe Dan innocent until he is proved otherwise."

"I didn't know that," Sarah said. "You mean it's against the law to think he took it?"

A faint smile crossed Miss Mulkey's face. "You might put it that way. Now, Sarah, go and wash your face. And try not to worry." Sarah got up to go, feeling much better, but Miss Mulkey's voice stopped her at the door. "Sarah, you realize that you can help to stop this gossip if you want to?"

Sarah turned a startled face. "I—I guess so," she said. "I'll try."

It was hard to keep her mind on school work that afternoon. In spite of what Miss Mulkey had said, she couldn't *quite* believe Danny was innocent. After all, someone had seen him take the ring. Someone had phoned and said so. *It was a sneaky thing to do,* Sarah thought. *A brave person would have walked right into Mr. Tuttle's office and told him.*

It was a relief to Sarah when Auditorium period came. She could stop thinking about Danny and his mother, and think about the play. There was a great deal to do, and the program was only two weeks away.

Sarah began by telling the cast that Mr. Scott would help them, and they broke into a cheer, except for Melanie, who curled her lip and said scornfully, "The janitor. What does he know?"

"He knows a lot more than you do, Melanie Rivers," Will said hotly, and Sarah had to intervene quickly before a real quarrel started.

"We still need a lot of things," she said, and read her list. June had a blue silk bedspread. Melvin's mother would lend some knitting. Wanda's great-uncle was a retired doctor, and could be counted on for a doctor's bag and stethoscope.

"And bring any nice toys you can find," Sarah said. "Collette's supposed to be rich, you know."

"Tell Sarah," Katie said to Betty Evans, "that I know where I can get all the costumes except Melanie's bed jacket and a suit for Will."

"Maybe I can borrow my mother's bed jacket," Sarah said. She really meant to say it right to Katie, but she found herself speaking to Betty instead.

"I think I can get a suit," Melvin Peterson said. "I'll ask my dad."

"Would you like a Japanese jewelry box?" June asked Sarah shyly. "I have one my aunt sent me. It's very pretty."

"Hey, yeah," Eddie crowed. "If she's so rich, she ought to have jewels. How about a diamond ring?

We could ask Danny Wade."

Melanie laughed, and Sarah caught her breath. Here was her chance to help stop the gossip, and she was almost afraid to take it. "There isn't any proof," she said unsteadily. "We don't know for sure that he took it."

The others stared at her, and Melanie cast a sidelong, laughing glance at Martha. "Oh, he did it, all right," she said.

Sarah was suddenly overcome by a conviction so absolute it was certainty. She *knew* who had made that phone call. She thought of Melanie laughing and saying, "Let's call people up." Of course it was Melanie. Hardly knowing what she was doing, she stood up and faced Melanie.

"Did you call Mr. Tuttle?" she demanded. "Did you tell him Danny took that ring?"

Melanie's eyes flew open, and then her gaze lowered. A slow, red flush mounted from her neck to her face. "Who says I did?" But she didn't look at Sarah.

"Did you?" Sarah asked again.

Melanie jerked her head up and tossed her hair. Her eyes were bright, almost as if she were going to cry.

"What if I did?" she cried. "He took it. I saw

him. Now, tell that if you want to, tattletale!"

She whirled and ran from the office, and after a stunned moment, Martha and Wanda ran after her. Wanda paused at the door, her plump face suffused with anger.

"Now you've made her cry," she said. "I hope you're happy."

7 / *Unhappy Melanie*

The days slipped along toward Thanksgiving.
Sarah ran home quickly after school now, because
her mother needed her. Mrs. Abbott had invited
all of Sarah's aunts and uncles and cousins to
Thanksgiving dinner, and the house was being
turned inside out in preparation. It was a good
excuse, Mrs. Abbott said, for a thorough house-
cleaning.

Sarah liked to help. She liked polishing the
windows until they shone, and tidying the linen
closet. She especially liked stuffing dates with
walnuts and rolling them in powdered sugar, and
peeling apples for the big kettle of mincemeat.

Sarah was to take two quarts of the mincemeat to school for the Thanksgiving baskets, and as she stirred the fragrant stuff, she hoped the mincemeat would go to someone she knew.

Helping at home served to keep her mind off school, and school wasn't comfortable these days. Everyone felt it, even the teachers. Nothing more had been said, officially, about Danny and the ring, and everyone had stopped talking about it. But Danny was even more isolated from the others than he had been before.

Sarah hated the atmosphere in the school. She wished Danny would admit taking the ring, and get it over with. She wished Melanie would tell Mr. Tuttle she had made the phone call.

Melanie had changed. From the moment Sarah faced her that day behind the stage, she had been different. It wasn't only that she dressed like the other girls, but she hardly talked to anyone anymore, not even Martha or Wanda. Her face was terribly still, and even at recess she stood against the wall with her hands in her coat pockets, staring at nothing. Worst of all, she had stopped acting.

She was still in the play. When they rehearsed during Auditorium period, she said her lines and did what she was supposed to do, but it was as lifeless and mechanical as someone reciting in class. Without her liveliness the play was dull, and Sarah didn't know what to do about it. She longed for a good talk with Katie, but Katie still wasn't speaking to her.

Mr. Scott had been as good as his word. He found some scenery behind the stage, and helped Eddie and Will set it up, so there was a window on one side and a door on the other, the way Sarah wanted it. He made a bed from two benches and some boards. He even found a big packing box, and showed Sarah how to paint it so that it looked like a dresser. Mrs. Abbott loaned some curtains, Wanda brought a rug, and Katie donated a lacy pillow. Every day the stage looked more and more like a rich girl's bedroom.

But what difference does it make, Sarah thought despairingly as she polished the best silver, *if the play itself isn't good?* Here it was, Saturday, and the program was Wednesday. She was trying as hard as she could, but the play simply wasn't interesting.

On Monday, Sarah walked to school slowly. She didn't particularly want to get there, and besides that, her arms were full. In a shopping bag she carried two dolls and her music box. Her arms were loaded with a white blanket, a stocking cap for Eddie, her father's black tie for Will, and her mother's ruffled bed jacket for Melanie.

"Hi, Sarah," Wanda greeted her at the fence. "Can I help you?" Gratefully, Sarah handed over the shopping bag. She was so worried about the play that she hardly noticed how much friendlier Wanda had been lately. Together, they went to the office and received permission to take their load to the auditorium.

"It looks simply beautiful," Wanda said when they had arranged the toys on the stage. "You've done an awfully good job, Sarah. You don't mind being in charge, do you? I'd be scared to death."

"I'm scared now," Sarah said. "I'm scared the play won't be good." She picked up the bedspread.

"I'm going to do the best *I* can," Wanda said stoutly. "Katie says—"

Sarah wasn't listening. "Look, Wanda." She crumpled the bedspread in the middle of the bed. "We'll have it sort of messy like this when the play starts, and then you can straighten it out. My mother does that when I'm sick."

"So does mine." Wanda walked over and jerked and smoothed the spread into place. She looked exactly like a mother.

"Oh, that's good," Sarah said. "You're getting

so much better, Wanda. Everyone is getting better except—" She bit back the name. It didn't help to talk about it. Wanda whirled around to face Sarah.

"Well, I think—" she began. But the bell rang, and Sarah ran to pull the curtain and hide the stage. She didn't hear what Wanda thought.

That afternoon they practiced on the stage with no one watching, while Miss Lane took the others to the lunchroom. The next day they would rehearse in front of the class. And Wednesday was the program. Lots and lots of parents would be there. It made Sarah nervous to realize that this was their last chance to get everything right.

"I'm going way to the back," she told the cast, "to be sure I can hear you."

She could hear them, and except for Melanie, they were better than ever before. Will remembered to keep his voice gruff, and he didn't laugh when he patted Melanie's head. Wanda bustled around looking worried and sounding cheerful. Even Eddie paid attention, and didn't try to be funny when he wasn't supposed to. And Katie, although she didn't have much to say, was excellent. She did little things, such as scuffing her toe and twisting her scarf, that made the play seem real.

But no matter how hard they tried, the play couldn't come alive while Melanie rattled through her lines as if she wished she were someplace else. When they were halfway through for the second time, Sarah couldn't stand it any longer.

"Melanie," she said angrily, walking down to the front row, "you aren't even trying. If you *couldn't* do it, I wouldn't care. But you can, and you *won't*."

Melanie sat up on the makeshift bed, her eyes blazing. Sarah was startled, almost frightened. Melanie looked like a cat ready to spring.

"I said I'd be in your old play," she said in a high voice, "and I'm in it. But you just leave me alone, Sarah Abbott. You just leave me alone." Springing to her feet, she stalked off the stage, while the others stood dumbfounded.

Sarah dropped into a front seat. Her knees were trembling. A moment later, Melanie marched out the door by the stage. She had her books in her arms. "Where are you going?" Sarah asked. Her voice was hardly more than a whisper.

Melanie turned to face her. "I'm going home," she said deliberately. "Since you're such a tattle-tale, I suppose you'll tell on me, but I don't care. I may be back tomorrow and then I may not." Her chin went up, and her lips trembled. "I may get sick." She tossed back her braids, and walked to the auditorium door. No one said anything. Sarah couldn't. Just as Melanie pushed open the big door, Sarah heard Katie's voice.

"That's all right, Sarah," Katie said loudly. "I know all the lines, and I can do it."

Melanie kept right on going. As soon as the door clanged shut, everyone began talking at once. Sarah sat where she was, confused and frightened. What would she do if Melanie didn't come back? Probably Katie did know the words, but she hadn't practiced. All at once, she realized Katie had spoken to her. She looked up eagerly, but Katie was talking to Wanda. Sarah sighed. It was only because Katie cared about the play. She didn't care about her.

That night at dinner, Sarah told her parents what had happened, hoping they could tell her what to do. They listened carefully, and then Mr. Abbott shook his head. "Poor kid," he said. "She's having a hard time, isn't she?" *Why, he means Melanie,* Sarah thought in amazement.

Mrs. Abbott looked seriously at Sarah. "Can you understand, dear, that Melanie is doing this because she's unhappy?"

"It doesn't excuse her!" Sarah said hotly.

"No, it doesn't," Mr. Abbott said. "You're quite right, Sarah. There's a difference between understanding and excusing. I don't advise you to excuse Melanie, but it won't hurt you to understand."

"Understanding won't help the play," Sarah wailed. "What if she doesn't come on Wednesday?"

"Then you'll have to put your faith in Katie," her father said.

Mrs. Abbott smiled reassuringly. "She'll be there. Her mother is staying home from work to see the play, so I'm sure Melanie will be there."

Sarah wished she were sure. She knew her mother had met Mrs. Rivers, and that they talked frequently on the telephone, but she hadn't met Melanie. She didn't know how easily Melanie could fool people. Melanie could pretend to be sick. Melanie could pretend anything, and you couldn't tell the difference.

When Sarah reached school that Tuesday morning, there was no sign of Melanie on the playground. When the first bell rang, and they all trooped upstairs to their lockers, she still hadn't come.

Sarah slid into her seat with a hollow feeling inside. Melanie wasn't coming. At the last minute, however, Melanie walked in. Head high, face pale, she took her seat, tossed back her braids and got out a book. Sarah sighed with relief. She didn't care anymore, she realized, whether Melanie tried to act or not, as long as she was there—as long as they didn't have to change everything at the last minute.

The dress rehearsal for the class that afternoon went better than Sarah had expected. Some things were missing. Eddie didn't have his ball, and Will had forgotten a black notebook again. They were quick and lively, however, except for Melanie. Sarah watched Miss Lane anxiously, but Miss Lane leaned her cheek against her hand, and although her eyes were turned toward the stage, she hardly seemed to see the play. Her face was weary, and her pretty hair was drawn back into a funny knot that made her look older. When the curtain finally closed, Miss Lane got to her feet and waited for the class to stop applauding.

"That will do nicely," she said, but she sounded as if she weren't really interested. Sarah had to blink to keep back tears. All those weeks and weeks of work, and all Miss Lane could say was that it would do nicely. "The program is at ten-thirty, as you know. You will be excused to come to the

auditorium at nine-thirty. Please come quietly."

She went on talking, giving instructions to the girls who were to usher. Sarah found herself getting angry, not for herself, but for the others. They had tried so hard. It wasn't fair not to tell them they were doing well. *Miss Lane doesn't care,* she thought. *She doesn't really care a bit about us.*

When the bell rang, Sarah gathered the cast together. Melanie slipped out, but the others clustered around her as she reminded them of the things they had forgotten, and told them *she* thought they had done beautifully. "It's going to be really good tomorrow," she said. "I know it is."

They stared at her silently. Then Eddie voiced what was in all their minds.

"What if Miss Movie-Star doesn't show up?"

Sarah smiled with more confidence than she felt. "Oh, she'll be here. Her mother's coming."

"But what if she doesn't?" This time it was Wanda.

Sarah took a breath. "Then Katie will be Collette, and you'll just have to skip Katie's part." They exchanged uneasy glances.

"Melanie will come," Sarah said desperately. "She's got to."

8 / A Day of Surprises

The sun shone like a good omen the next morning. It glinted off the coffeepot, and turned Sarah's scrambled eggs to pure gold. But Sarah's stomach churned, and in spite of her mother's urging, she couldn't eat more than a bite.

Mrs. Abbott removed Sarah's full plate with a grim face. "Someday," she said, "I must have a talk with your Miss Lane."

"She wouldn't care," Sarah said, surprising herself. "I don't think she likes to teach school."

Mrs. Abbott stopped dead still. "Perhaps you're right. That may very well be it."

"Besides," Sarah said. "I'm really glad she decided to have the play. And I'm really glad she left it all to me. I mean, it's been terrible, but I'm glad."

Mrs. Abbott shook her head, but Mr. Abbott, coming in the kitchen, laughed. "Spoken like a true trouper," he said, and dropped a hand on Sarah's shoulder. "Nervous?"

"Terribly," Sarah confessed.

Her father nodded, as if this were only to be expected, and drew a paper sack out of his pocket. "I have something for you." From the sack he took a package of safety pins. "The true worth of a director," he said solemnly, "lies in whether or not she has enough safety pins on opening night."

"Only it's opening morning," Sarah giggled.

Mr. Abbott waved his hand. "The difference is immaterial." He handed her the pins and sat down at the table. "I won't wish you luck, because that's bad luck. I'll say, 'break a leg.' " Sarah laughed again, and then watched in amazement as her father opened the paper and began to turn the pages in a leisurely fashion.

"Aren't you going to work?" Her eyes widened and she gasped, "Are you coming to the play? Are you?"

Mr. Abbott folded his paper and looked at her. "What made you think I wouldn't?"

Sarah jumped up to hug him. "Oh, thank you. Thank you! And you'll tell me the truth, won't you? About whether it's good or not?"

"I'll tell you the truth," he promised.

Sarah ran out into the golden morning. Far away down the hill, a blue haze hung over the woods, and the air held the scent of burning leaves. She sniffed in delight. Oh, it looked like Thanksgiving. It smelled like Thanksgiving. She ran happily down the block.

The closer she got to school, however, the more her happiness seemed to slip away. Maybe Melanie wouldn't be there. And maybe Katie would forget the words, and make the others so nervous they'd forget. Her mind leaped to other problems. *How about Will's notebook? Will Eddie have his ball?* She was dead certain that Wanda would forget to bring more powder for her hair.

She was at her desk furiously scribbling a list so that she wouldn't forget anything, when Miss Mulkey rapped for attention. Only then did Sarah look up and see that Melanie's desk was empty.

For a moment she couldn't breathe. It was unbelievable. Never had Sarah seen a space so blank as the empty seat across the aisle. Oh, how could Melanie do this?

She tried to think of something to do. Maybe she could phone Mrs. Rivers. Then she sank back in her seat. No, it wouldn't do any good. Everything depended on Katie. She wanted terribly to turn around and look at Katie, but Miss Mulkey's eye was on her, and she didn't dare.

When Miss Mulkey dismissed the ones who were to be in the program, Sarah looked back at those who were left, and saw Danny Wade slumped in his seat, staring at the window as if he'd like to jump out and run. Sarah really didn't blame him. It must be awful to be treated as if you didn't exist.

They had promised Miss Mulkey they wouldn't talk in the hall, and they didn't, but Sarah could feel the frightened eyes turned her way. She had to say something. At the door of the auditorium, she turned.

"It's going to be all right," she said in a fierce whisper. "Katie can do it. We'll go over it while we're getting ready."

No one answered. Katie looked pale and uncertain. With a sigh, Sarah opened the door and led the way in.

The auditorium was full of children and confusion. The eighth-grade boy who was going to announce walked back and forth, pulling at his tie. Two or three girls stood by the piano with music in their hands. A lot of little first graders danced up and down in their underwear, while their mothers pulled pilgrim costumes over their heads. At the back, three boys in feathered head-dresses brandished tomahawks. Miss Lane, looking beautiful again in her pink dress, dashed about talking first to one person and then another. When she saw Sarah and the others, she smiled brightly.

"Can you take care of your little group, Sarah?" she asked.

"Yes, Miss Lane," Sarah said. She didn't smile back, because she knew the smile wasn't really for her. It was because the mothers were there.

Soberly, she led the way backstage, wishing she could think of something helpful to say. If she could convince them that the play might still be good, maybe it would be. She glanced at Katie's set face. *She's scared,* Sarah thought. *She doesn't want to do it.* Angrier with Melanie than she had ever been before, she gave the door to the office a hard shove, and then stood rooted in surprise, her mouth gaping.

There, in a corner, sat Melanie. She was already dressed in the white nightgown and blue bed jacket. Her hair, brushed and gleaming, was tied with a blue ribbon. How beautiful she was, but how pale and sad.

Sarah stepped forward, and Wanda dashed past her. "Oh, Melanie, we're so glad you're here," she exclaimed. "We thought you weren't coming, and we got so scared."

Melanie never flicked an eyelash. She might have been a statue. Sarah swallowed, and found her voice. "Come on," she said. "We have to get ready."

In the excitement of getting into their costumes and putting on rouge and powder, Melanie was almost forgotten. Sarah's safety pins were put to good use. The turned-up legs of Melvin's father's trousers came down and had to be pinned in place. Wanda ripped her apron string in her flurry, and Katie wanted to pin her sweater together so that she would look poor. The room was buzzing with noise when Miss Lane put her head in at the door.

"Quiet, please!" she said sharply. "The audience is coming in." Sarah wet her lips nervously. In the sudden stillness, she could hear a murmur of voices from the auditorium. "The play is the last thing on the program, and until it starts I want absolute silence back here. Do you hear?" She looked at them one at a time as if she were expecting to find fault. "Do your best," she said, and went out. Eddie stuck out his tongue at the closing door, and Martha giggled nervously.

"I don't care what she says," Sarah said in a whisper. "It's going to be *good*."

They sat down to wait, fidgeting. Eddie swung his feet incessantly, June clasped and unclasped her hands, and Katie's lips moved. Wanda kept patting her hair, and at every pat, a puff of powder flew up. Sarah looked at Melanie, who hadn't moved or spoken since they came in. Her stillness was frightening. Sarah reminded herself of all the trouble Melanie had caused, but the sight of that white face hurt her inside. At last, she got up slowly, and crossed the room.

"Melanie," she said softly. "I'm sorry I told on you. I didn't mean to. I didn't know my mother was going to tell your mother." Two tears appeared on Melanie's lashes, but she didn't turn her head or answer. Sarah shifted uneasily. "I'm glad you're in the play," she stammered. "I hope you'll . . ." It was no use. Nothing she said sounded right. She put out her hand tentatively, touched Melanie's shoulder, and went back to her seat.

The door opened, and the announcer put his head in. "You're on next," he whispered, and disappeared.

The cast stood up, looking at Sarah and at each other with wide, excited eyes. Sarah tried to smile as they filed out slowly to take their places, Melanie last of all. Sarah sat down. Then she stood up. She couldn't wait in there. She had to see it.

Softly, she crept to the backstage door and listened. A girl was singing. When she finished, and the applause began, Sarah opened the door and slipped out. The auditorium was filled to the very back. By the door, a huge table held piles and piles of jars and cans and sacks. A line of boys stood by the back wall. Sarah scurried to where one of the ushers leaned against a side wall. She saw Miss Lane frowning at her from the opposite wall, but she didn't care. It was her play, and she had to see it.

The announcer came through the curtains with a paper in his hands. "Our program will end," he said, "with an original play by two students from Miss Mulkey's class, Sarah Abbott and Katherine Donnelly. The play is called *Thanksgiving for Collette*. The characters are—"

He began to read the names, but Sarah was too

nervous to listen. Her eyes searched the crowd for her mother and father, but she couldn't find them. Across the room, Miss Lane stood against the wall as if she expected to be shot. In the third row, Miss Mulkey leaned forward, brightly expectant.

"The scene," the announcer finished, "is Collette's bedroom."

The curtain slowly opened and Sarah caught her breath. It looked so real—the bed, the dresser, the toys, the rug on the floor—and especially the sunlight from the lamp that Mr. Scott had fastened outside the window. Against the pillows on the bed lay a still figure. Red hair rippled against the white. For a long time the figure didn't move, and then the head turned, restlessly.

"Mama," a fretful voice called. "Mama, I'm thirsty."

A lump rose in Sarah's throat and she pressed her hands against her mouth. Melanie was coming through. Melanie was going to be wonderful.

The wall shook a little as the door opened and Wanda bustled in with a glass of water, her plump figure encased in a big pink apron. She straightened the bed and shook up the pillows and told Melanie that the doctor was coming. Then the children appeared outside the window, laughing and throwing snowballs. Sarah had made the snow-balls out of cotton and bits of tinsel, and they looked fine, she thought. Melanie watched the children, and then all at once, she turned her head away and began to cry, quietly. She had never done that before. Sarah hadn't told her to do it. It made Sarah's eyes sting with tears.

Will came in as the doctor, looking very gruff. He put a thermometer in Melanie's mouth, took her pulse, and listened with his stethoscope. Then he patted her head and wrote something in his little black notebook. Sarah was relieved to see the notebook. She had forgotten to ask if he had it.

All this time, you could hear the children out-side, laughing and playing. Now and then someone ran past the window. Katie stopped in front of it, shivering and trying to pin her sweater tighter. Will pulled Wanda down near the audience and told her he was sorry, but her little girl would never walk again. Wanda wiped her eyes and said it wasn't going to be a happy Thanksgiving. Mel-anie propped herself up on her elbow.

"Mama, is it cold outside?" she asked. Wanda said it was very cold. "Then why isn't that little girl wearing a cap?" Melanie demanded, pointing at Katie, who was shivering outside the window.

Wanda said maybe she didn't have a cap. "Give me my blue cap, Mama," Melanie said.

Wanda went to the dresser and got the cap. Of course she had to pretend to open the drawer, because it wasn't real, but it didn't matter, because everyone was watching Melanie. Melanie took the cap and asked Wanda to open the window. That had to be pretend, too, because it wasn't the kind you could open. Melanie threw the cap out, and Sarah's throat tightened because you could see she was too weak to throw hard. "There, little girl," she called. "Wear that."

Outside the window, Katie caught the cap, stared at it, smiled broadly, and pulled it down over her hair. "Thank you, whoever you are," she called and ran out of sight. Melanie fell back against the pillows, Wanda wiped her eyes with her apron, and the curtain closed. It was the end of Scene One.

The applause was loud and enthusiastic. Even Sarah applauded. She didn't need her father to tell her it was good. She *knew* it was. But it was mostly Melanie, she admitted. Without Melanie, it wouldn't have been much of a play.

She glanced across the auditorium, and saw Mrs. Rivers in the fifth row, sitting very straight beside a brown-haired man, and looking proud and excited. Beyond Mrs. Rivers, Miss Lane slumped against the wall. Sarah was certain she hadn't even looked at the play. As Sarah watched, the big door near Miss Lane slowly opened. A young man put his head in, and then stepped inside. He looked around quickly until he saw Miss Lane. Sarah stared, fascinated. He was tall and nice looking, and there was something expectant, almost scared, in his face. With an expression that was like Eddie's when he was up to mischief, the young man slid along the wall until he stood next to Miss Lane. She didn't notice him. His hand touched hers. Miss Lane started and looked up. Her eyes widened. Then with a movement that was like a glad cry, she caught the young man's hand and held it against her cheek. He whispered, and Miss Lane whispered back, smiling. Sarah, standing with her mouth open, suddenly understood a great many things she hadn't understood before.

Then the announcer appeared, and Sarah's eyes went back to the stage. "Scene Two," he said. "Two weeks later."

The curtain jerked open, and the play began again. In this scene it appeared that Collette had been making toys and scarfs and sweaters, and dropping them out the window for the children. She was better, too, because now she sat in a chair. But, as she told her toy dog, she was very lonely. Then Wanda came in and asked if she was ready for her Thanksgiving dinner. This was the best part of the play, and Sarah clasped her hands in excitement.

Wanda threw open the door, and all the children trooped in, thanking Collette for the gifts and asking her to be their friend. Collette grew so excited that she stood up. She actually stood up, and even took a faltering step! The children cheered, and Eddie not only turned the somersault he had rehearsed, but walked on his hands as well. Will came back and said the children had cured Collette when he couldn't. Melanie had the last line.

"This is the happiest Thanksgiving of my life," she said. "I'll never forget it." Melanie's voice broke, and there were real tears on her cheeks.

The curtain closed, and for a moment there wasn't a sound. Then the audience began to clap wildly. Sarah clapped, too. She forgot completely that she and Katie had written the play. She was clapping for the actors, especially Melanie.

After that, everything was confusion. Sarah ran backstage where her hand was shaken a dozen

times; she was patted and hugged and kissed. Children and parents milled around her and the cast, telling them over and over that it had been a wonderful performance. Sarah's parents kissed her and told her she should be proud. Sarah wanted to tell Melanie how well she had done, but when the crowd thinned out enough so that she could, Melanie was gone.

"She went home with her mother," Wanda said. "I don't know if she's coming back this afternoon or not."

"She has to," Sarah said. "We're not supposed to leave until three o'clock."

"I know," Wanda said, looking puzzled. "But she took her books and everything."

There wasn't time to wonder about it. Costumes had to be changed and the stage cleaned up. When Sarah went behind the curtain, she found Mr. Scott pulling out nails and removing the scenery. It made Sarah sad to see the bedroom she had worked so hard to create torn apart in a minute, but it was necessary. After a sigh or two, she began gathering up toys and folding the bedspread. The others helped, and for a few minutes it was all bustle and work. In the midst of it, Will dashed up to Sarah.

"My folks are waiting to take me home for

lunch," he gasped, barely stopping. He thrust his black notebook into Sarah's hands. "I borrowed this from Miss Lane. It goes in the desk out there." He nodded toward the auditorium, and pounded off.

"I'll put it back," Sarah called after him. In a minute Wanda appeared, her arms loaded.

"I've got to go," she said. "I promised my mom I'd bring these things home at noon. You'd better go, Sarah, or you won't get any lunch."

She dashed off and Sarah looked around. She seemed to be all alone. The scenery was gone, and Mr. Scott had carried the make-believe dresser to the basement. Two benches were all that remained of the bed. But the stage was not tidy, as she had promised Miss Lane it would be. Sarah ran to the edge and looked at the clock. Ten minutes of the lunch period had already passed. She was supposed to buy her lunch, but if she didn't hurry, the line would be closed.

Hurriedly, she pushed chairs and benches into place, snatched up a forgotten jacket and cap, and ran through the dark hall to Miss Lane's office. What a sight met her! Chairs were pushed every which way, there was powder on the floor and on the desk, and bits of costumes were strewn about.

Feeling deserted and very hungry, Sarah set about straightening the room. When she had finished, she ran for the door, hoping the nice lady in the lunchroom would still give her some lunch.

At that moment, she remembered Will's notebook, still lying on the edge of the stage. Running back, she caught it up and hurried to the desk, which had been pushed against the wall. Impatiently, she jerked the drawer open. She must have jerked too hard, because the drawer flew out in her hands, spilling its contents over the floor. Pencils rolled, erasers bounced, paper clips scattered.

Tears filled Sarah's eyes. She wasn't going to get any lunch at all. Dropping to her knees, she began to pick up the fallen objects, sniffling a little as she arranged the pencils in the tray. It was too late to hurry now.

It hardly seemed possible that one drawer could hold so much. Sarah found a hankie and a compact and dozens of pages of Miss Lane's pink notepaper. Her knees grew grimy and sore as she crawled about fishing pencils and crayons and even a slingshot from under the seats. At last, she had them all and she carefully stood up with the filled drawer in her hands. No, not quite all. Something shiny, far out in the middle of the floor, caught her eye. Setting the drawer on the desk, she went wearily to get it. For a long moment she stared, and then slowly, incredulously, she knelt to pick up the glittering object. It was Miss Lane's diamond ring.

9 / *The Truth Is Told*

For a long time, Sarah crouched and stared at the ring, glowing in her hand. *It must have been in the drawer,* she thought. *It must have been in the drawer all along.* Slowly, she got to her feet, holding the ring tightly. She looked over the empty auditorium as she remembered that day.

The desk had been in the middle of the room then, in front of the stage, and yes—the drawer was open. Miss Lane must have taken the ring off just before the class came in. She must have taken the ring off and put it in the drawer, and then forgotten and thought she had put it in her purse. Or else, Sarah thought, remembering that on that day

Miss Lane had come to school with reddened eyes, she didn't see where she dropped the ring. Maybe she really thought it had gone in her purse.

Then Danny *hadn't* taken it. Sarah found herself smiling. She was glad. Oh, she was terribly glad. Now Mrs. Wade wouldn't have to cry anymore. Sarah had to tell Mr. Tuttle at once. Leaving the drawer where it was, she sped into the hall and clattered down the stairs. As she reached the office door, Mr. Tuttle stepped out, frowning.

"Sarah," he asked sternly, "what are you doing here at lunchtime?"

The question confused Sarah. She had made up her mind what to say when she got to the office, but the words floated away. Silently, she held out her hand and uncurled her fingers.

"What's that?" Mr. Tuttle bent nearer. "Well, I'll be—" he breathed. Taking the ring from Sarah's hand, he turned it in his fingers as if he couldn't believe his eyes. Then his hand came down on Sarah's shoulder, and his eyes bored into hers. "Where did you get it, Sarah?"

His look frightened Sarah, but she gulped and found her voice. "In the auditorium," she said. "In Miss Lane's drawer. Danny didn't take it, Mr. Tuttle. It was there all the time." Mr. Tuttle continued to stare at her. His head moved up and down slowly, and then he jerked it toward the office.

"Come in," he said, "and let's talk about this."

He was taking her in the office! Sarah gasped in dismay and stepped backwards. Then she rushed forward and caught him by the arm.

"Mr. Tuttle," she cried. "It *was* there all the time. It really was."

"We'll talk about it inside," Mr. Tuttle said, and propelled her by the shoulder past Mrs. Benson and into his private office. Sarah had never been there before. The unfamiliarity of the book-lined room, and the shame of being in it, made her cry.

It was a bad ten minutes. Mr. Tuttle told her to wipe her eyes, and then he questioned her gravely. Over and over he made her tell what she remembered about the day the ring was lost, and how she found it. Everything Sarah told him was the absolute truth, but being asked again and again made her so nervous that her face grew hot, the tears flowed, and she felt exactly as if she were lying.

She was sure Mr. Tuttle didn't believe her. And Sarah herself could see that it was the kind of story you would tell if you had taken the ring, and gotten scared, and wanted to give it back. She stared despairingly at the desk, where Mr. Tuttle turned the ring over and over in silence. Finally, he put it in an envelope and shut it up in a drawer.

"Sarah—" Mr. Tuttle leaned across the desk. "Do you know how Danny came to be suspected of taking this ring?" Sarah flushed and hung her head. "We received a phone call," Mr. Tuttle went on. "An anonymous phone call. Do you know what that means?" Sarah shook her head without looking up. "It means that whoever called wasn't brave enough to give her name." He stood up, pushing back his chair. "Sarah, do you know who made that phone call?"

Hot tears pushed at Sarah's eyes again. She didn't know if Mr. Tuttle was accusing her of making the phone call or asking her to tell on Melanie. Either way, there was nothing she could say. And she wasn't sure Melanie had done it. Melanie said she had seen Danny take the ring and that wasn't true. Maybe she hadn't phoned either. Mr. Tuttle leaned on his desk, waiting.

"I don't know," Sarah murmured. "I'm not sure."

"What?" Mr. Tuttle leaned closer. Sarah tried again.

"I'm not sure." She looked up at him pleadingly. "Please don't make me tell."

Something odd happened to Mr. Tuttle's face. He sighed and straightened.

"All right, Sarah. We'll leave it at that." He looked at his watch. "The bell is going to ring in a minute. Go to your class." As Sarah slipped out, she saw him sit down at his desk, and stare at his empty hands.

She stepped into a hall full of children, some of them strolling, some trying not to run, and all of them talking. As she turned toward the stairs, someone pulled at her arm. It was Eddie, his eyes shining.

"Hey, Sarah," he said. "We were pretty good, weren't we? My mom said it was the best school play she ever saw."

"What?" Sarah blinked at him. The play seemed a million years ago. "Yes, you were really good, Eddie."

"What's the matter with you?" Eddie asked. He glanced back along the hall. "Were you in the *office*? What were you doing in the office?" Sarah began to walk more quickly, but Eddie stayed right beside her. "You've been crying," he said accusingly. "What happened?"

"Nothing," Sarah said sharply, but Eddie was persistent.

"Something did too happen," he insisted. "Your eyes are all red, and you're acting funny. Who made you cry?" He swelled out his thin shoulders. "You just tell me, and I'll fix them."

"Oh, Eddie." Sarah turned, half laughing, half crying. "If you must know, I found Miss Lane's ring."

Eddie stopped short, and his mouth dropped open. "Gee," he breathed.

Sarah left him there, and hurried upstairs to her room. Miss Mulkey smiled at her. "Sarah," she called. Sarah stopped reluctantly. "Congratulations, Sarah. The play was well written and beautifully done."

"Thank you, Miss Mulkey," Sarah said. Another time Miss Mulkey's praise would have meant a great deal to her, but now it seemed unreal. The play was over. The only real thing was that Mr. Tuttle probably thought Sarah had taken Miss Lane's ring.

All afternoon she watched the door, feeling desolate and scared, expecting at any moment to be ordered back to the office. Everyone else was in a holiday mood, even Miss Mulkey, who read them a Thanksgiving story, and gave them an extra-long recess. Sarah hid at the top of the steps, rather than go out on the playground, where she was certain Eddie was telling everyone that she had been crying in the office. Eddie couldn't keep anything to himself.

A few minutes later, Katie marched up the steps with a determined face. Sarah turned her back. It wasn't long before Katie came back and took Martha's arm, and dragged her up the steps and into the school, talking earnestly. Sarah watched listlessly.

"I guess Melanie went home," Wanda said, coming up to Sarah with a worried face. Sarah looked out over the playground and realized for the first time that Melanie wasn't there. It didn't seem to matter.

"I guess so," she said.

Wanda took Sarah's arm. Her eyes were bright and indignant. "Sarah, do you know what Eddie is saying? He's saying that Mr. Tuttle probably—"

Before she could finish, Miss Mulkey blew her whistle and recess was over.

When they were back in their room, Miss Mulkey suggested that they might like to make Thanksgiving place cards for their mothers. Sarah didn't want to make place cards. She would rather have studied something hard, so hard she couldn't think.

"Monitors," Miss Mulkey said, "pass out art paper and crayons."

Sarah was in charge of crayons. Slowly, she went to the big cupboard and lifted down the heavy box. When the door opened suddenly, she nearly dropped it, but it was Katie, who went straight to Miss Mulkey and whispered to her. Miss Mulkey looked down with puzzled eyes.

"Now?" she asked. Katie nodded. Her braids bobbed and her eyes were wide. She looked scared and excited. "Very well. Sarah, put the crayons back. I'll be out of the room for a few minutes, class. Please read the next story in your reading books." Her eyes swept the class, reminding them to be quiet, and then she said in a voice that was even brisker than usual, "Daniel Wade, will you come with me, please?"

Sarah gasped. Eddie's eyes flew to hers in astonishment. All around the room, knowing glances were exchanged, and Danny's face looked utterly defeated as he got to his feet and walked to the door. Angrily, Sarah thrust the crayon box onto its shelf and dropped to her seat.

So Mr. Tuttle still thought Danny did it! It wasn't fair, when she'd *told* him. Why hadn't he believed her? She was furious with Mr. Tuttle, and furious with Katie for looking so pleased as she followed Miss Mulkey and Danny from the room. Most of all, she was furious with Melanie. It was her lies that had caused all the trouble.

It seemed a long time before the door opened and Miss Mulkey stepped in. "Children," she said in an odd voice, "Mr. Tuttle is here."

Miss Mulkey's face was calm, but Sarah could have sworn she was excited about something. Smoothing his hair over his bald spot, Mr. Tuttle walked to the front of the room and cleared his throat. His face said that he had something important to tell them, and Sarah wished he would say it quickly.

He waited, however, until Katie and Martha had scuttled to their seats and folded their hands on their desks. Then he cleared his throat again.

"I have an announcement to make," he said, "and I want your full attention. You all know that a valuable ring has been missing, and that we have been very much concerned about it. It looked as if it had been stolen." He paused, and Sarah thought she would die of impatience. Why couldn't he *tell* them?

"Today, the ring was found," Mr. Tuttle said. "It had been misplaced. It was not stolen."

Relief flowed through Sarah. Mr. Tuttle had believed her. He really had. She heard a soft, wondering murmur from the class, and she was suddenly filled with such joy that she wanted to jump up and dance. It was over. All the suspicion, all the fear was over. She felt as if the sun had come out and flooded the room with light.

"I'm as pleased about this as you are," Mr. Tuttle said, smiling first at Sarah, and then at the class. "I found it hard to believe such a theft could occur at Roseland School, and I'm deeply relieved to find out it didn't. Now, let me tell you how such a mistake came to be made."

He leaned against Miss Mulkey's desk and told them about the day the ring had been lost, and how Miss Lane had put it in her desk by mistake, and how, when she couldn't find it in her purse, she thought it had been stolen. "Miss Lane has asked me to apologize to this class," Mr. Tuttle said. "She realizes that she should have searched more thoroughly before she made such an accusation." There was something in his tone that made Sarah wonder what he had said to Miss Lane.

Then Mr. Tuttle described how Sarah had

found the ring and brought it to the office. He smiled at her as he spoke. Miss Mulkey nodded approvingly, Mary Weston turned around and beamed, and Eddie patted Sarah's back. She felt her face grow hot. It was all very pleasant, but embarrassing, because after all she had only found the ring by accident.

"And now," Mr. Tuttle said, "we come to the saddest part of this whole affair. An innocent person has been suspected. You all know who I mean."

The room grew still. When Mr. Tuttle spoke again, his voice was so low and serious that it made Sarah feel like crying. "That boy has had a hard time. No one wanted to play games with him, or be his friend. He knew everyone thought he was a thief. I've apologized to him, and to his mother, but apologies can't make up for what's happened. All we can do now is let him know we're sorry, and that we are his friends."

Sarah's throat tightened. She knew how Danny must have felt. Then in the stillness, Katie's clear voice said earnestly, "Oh, *yes*, Mr. Tuttle. We'll try."

"Very well, then," Miss Mulkey said. She opened the classroom door, and there stood Danny. He was frowning hard, but a half-sheepish smile tugged at the corners of his mouth.

151

"Hooray for Dan," Eddie called out, and suddenly everyone was clapping, and laughing, and jumping to their feet. Sarah smiled and smiled and clapped her hands so hard they stung. When she saw Danny's frown disappear, and his mouth stretch into a grin, she felt so happy that she wanted to hug everyone.

"That's enough," Miss Mulkey said finally in the crisp voice that didn't deceive Sarah one bit anymore. "That's quite enough. Take your seats, everyone. Take your seat, Dan."

Danny's grin flashed at her as he walked to his seat with his chin up. Will Stevens leaned over to slap Danny's shoulder, and Miss Mulkey shook her head at him, but her mouth was soft and the hand she raised for silence trembled slightly. *She cares,* Sarah thought with a rush of warmth for thin, severe Miss Mulkey. *She really cares about us.*

153

10 / Friends Again

Sarah was the last to leave the school that day. There was so much to talk about, and everyone wanted to talk to Sarah. As she pulled on her coat to run after them, she felt warm and satisfied. She had so many friends. Then she saw Danny Wade, all alone, hurrying down the stairs.

"Good-bye, Danny," Sarah called. "Have a nice Thanksgiving."

Danny jerked his head up, and for an instant his eyes met hers. He reddened and pulled at the sleeves of his jacket. "Yeah," he said, not looking at her. "You, too."

He turned and ran, but as he reached the landing, he looked up again and grinned at Sarah. His smile was nice, and it made him look so different that Sarah felt confused, and the red rushed to her cheeks. "Good-bye," she called again.

"Now there's a boy who feels a lot better in his mind tonight," a voice said, and Sarah whirled to see Mr. Scott with his big mop.

"Oh, yes," Sarah said. "Good-bye, Mr. Scott. And thank you for helping me with the play."

He nodded and smiled. "That's what I'm here for."

It isn't, of course, Sarah thought as she ran down the stairs. Mr. Scott was there to keep the school clean and warm. But he was so nice.

She had reached the landing when she saw someone below, and stopped in embarrassment. Miss Lane's face was set in determined lines, and her arms were loaded with books and records and the white sweater she always kept in her office. *How odd,* Sarah thought, *to take all those things home for Thanksgiving.* Then she saw the tall young man and *he* was carrying Miss Lane's phonograph.

Suddenly, Sarah was sure Miss Lane was leaving for good, and that she was going to marry the tall young man. But how funny to leave and get married in the middle of the year. Teachers didn't do that. Still, Sarah thought as she ran down the stairs and pushed open the big doors, Miss Lane never had seemed much like a teacher.

Outside, Sarah stopped uncertainly. Katie was sitting on the steps. Her arms were wrapped around her knees, and the late sun shone on her face.

"I was waiting for you," she said with a perfectly natural smile. "Do you want to walk home together?"

"Oh, yes," Sarah said.

It was so nice to have Katie fall into step beside her, so nice to see those yellow braids bobbing. Katie acted as if there had never been any trouble between them, but Sarah couldn't keep quiet. "I'm *so* glad you aren't mad at me anymore," she said.

Katie gave her a sober look. "I was only mad for a few days. For weeks and weeks, I've been wanting to be friends, only I didn't know how to start."

"Neither did I," Sarah exclaimed, and they both laughed. Then a thought struck Sarah. "I should have been the one to start, Katie. I was the one who was wrong."

"No, you weren't." Katie frowned and kicked at the sidewalk. "I *was* jealous of Melanie. I almost hated her, because she was so pretty and had such pretty clothes, and because you wanted to be best friends with her."

"I didn't want to be *best* friends."

"Didn't you?"

Sarah shook her head and linked her arm through Katie's. "Listen, Katie," she said and hesitated. She knew what she wanted to say, but not how to say it. "I did like Melanie because she was pretty. But you're pretty, too, in another way, and anyway, with you it doesn't matter, because—because—" She ran out of words. "It was awfully nice of you, Katie, to offer to do the part without any practice."

Katie looked at Sarah in surprise. "Well, some-one had to."

They crossed the street in silence, and then Sarah asked something she was dying to know. "Where did you go today, Katie? Did you go to the office?"

Katie nodded and reddened. Sarah waited. After a moment, Katie stopped, her face stubborn and defiant.

"You might as well know. I told on Melanie." Sarah gasped. "Well, I had to. Eddie was going around saying that you'd been crying in the office, and that you'd found the ring, and that probably Mr. Tuttle thought you took it. And I knew you didn't."

"How did you know that?"

"Well, you wouldn't," Katie said simply. "So I went to tell Mr. Tuttle that, but he already knew it. Then he asked me who made the phone call and—I just told him."

"Because of me?" Sarah asked slowly.

"Kind of. But mostly because it was the truth. And it was important."

Sarah glanced at her friend. "How do you know it was the truth? After all—"

"Because Martha was there when she did it," Katie said unexpectedly. "She knew Melanie made the whole thing up, so I got her to go in and tell Mr. Tuttle, too." She looked at Sarah anxiously. "You *have* to tell sometimes, Sarah, when it's important."

Sarah nodded. "I was just thinking," she said, "that you're a lot braver than I am." Katie turned red again, but she looked pleased.

They talked all the way to Sarah's house. There was so much catching up to do. Sarah had to tell Katie the interesting news of Miss Lane and her young man, and how they'd left school with all her books and records. Katie had to tell Sarah the nice things everyone in the play had said about her. They had to discuss Danny Wade and how he would act if they were friendly to him. When they

158

reached Sarah's big fir, they hadn't begun to run out of talk; but it didn't matter. They had all the time in the world now.

"Can you come in?" Sarah asked.

Katie nodded. "If I call my mother, I probably can."

Sarah looked down. She had one more question to ask, and it embarrassed her to ask it. "Do you like Betty Evans a lot?"

"Of course I do." Katie smiled broadly at Sarah. "And so do you. You know you do."

Sarah had to laugh, because it was true. "Let's go in," she said happily, and caught Katie's hand.

In the kitchen they found not only Mrs. Abbott, but Mr. Abbott. He was fixing a toaster, but he dropped his tools when they came in, and stood up. "Hail, the conquering heroes come," he said. If either of Sarah's parents were surprised to see Katie, they didn't show it.

Mrs. Abbott hugged them both. "The play was splendid," she said.

"Yes, it was," Mr. Abbott said, and sat down with his tools again. "It was short, full of feeling, and to the point." His eyes rested on Sarah. "You were especially fortunate in your leading actress."

"Wasn't she good?" Sarah said eagerly.

"Indeed she was. That little girl has a rare talent, and real magnetism."

"I'm afraid that won't be enough to make her happy," Mrs. Abbott sighed.

Sarah looked at Katie, and Katie looked at Sarah. "You tell," Katie said.

So while Katie made her phone call, Sarah began the story of the afternoon. She had her parents' full attention. After the first sentence, Mr. Abbott forgot his work and leaned forward, asking a question now and then when Sarah left out some important point. Mrs. Abbott interrupted once to ask in a horrified voice, "Didn't you eat any lunch at all, Sarah?"

"She didn't have a chance," Katie said, coming back from the phone.

"Go on with your story," Sarah's mother said, but as Sarah talked and Katie interrupted, she bustled about the kitchen. When they got to the part about Mr. Tuttle coming to their classroom, she set two steaming mugs of hot chocolate and a plate of sandwiches in front of them. Sarah took a bite of sandwich. It tasted heavenly.

"I think you had better tell the rest, Katie," Mr. Abbott said. "Our reporter seems to be occupied with mundane matters."

So Katie told the rest. When she had finished Mrs. Abbott took a deep breath. "Well, this was quite a day," she said, and glanced ruefully at her husband. "You know, I feel guilty about Danny Wade. I've been as bad as the children. I always thought that boy was up to no good."

Mr. Abbott turned to the girls. "Did Mr. Tuttle say anything about Melanie?"

"No, he didn't," Katie said indignantly. "He didn't even mention the phone call."

"He didn't need to," Sarah said. "Everyone knew about it, anyway. It's going to be awful for Melanie next Monday."

Sarah's parents exchanged glances. "Melanie won't be there next Monday," Mrs. Abbott said.

"She's going home to California," Mr. Abbott added.

Sarah and Katie stared at them incredulously. Melanie leaving? It hardly seemed possible.

"Why?" Sarah asked. "Is it because of the ring and everything?"

"Oh, no," Mrs. Abbott said with a smile. "It's a much nicer reason. Her father has come for them, and they are all going home together."

There was a silence as the girls digested this surprising news. Then Katie nodded and said,

161

"Well, it's a good thing. She only caused trouble."

That's true, Sarah thought, *but it isn't the whole truth.* Melanie had made the play a success. And even if she hadn't meant it to happen that way, Danny Wade was going to have a lot more friends than he'd ever had before. "It seems so awful," she said slowly, "for her to go away thinking no one liked her at all."

"Hardly anyone did," Katie said bluntly. "I didn't."

"I think I did," Sarah said. "I mean, I didn't like hardly anything she *did,* but I liked *her.* She wasn't ordinary."

"No, she wasn't ordinary," Mr. Abbott agreed.

Mrs. Abbott smoothed Sarah's hair. "Fascinating is the word you're looking for, I believe. Melanie *is* fascinating, and that may be part of the reason she's had such a hard time." She sighed, and smiled at Katie. "It's lonely, you know, being different. I wonder if Melanie wasn't searching for friendship and attention. She went about it the wrong way, I know, but perhaps it was the only way she knew."

Katie stared into her cup. "Maybe," she said grudgingly.

"I wish I'd had a chance to say good-bye to her,"

Sarah said. "I didn't even get to tell her how good she was in the play."

"You could run down there now," her mother suggested.

"Will you go with me?" Sarah asked Katie.

Katie thought a minute and nodded. "I'll go," she said, "and I'll tell her she was good in the play, because she was. But I won't tell her I'm sorry she's leaving, because I'm not."

Mr. Abbott leaned back in his chair, and laughed. "Katie, Katie," he said. "You're the salt of the earth. Don't let anyone ever teach you to compromise, Katie, or I'll feel that the props have been pulled out from under me."

The apartments, when they reached them, appeared quiet, almost deserted. As they turned into the walk, Sarah felt her courage ooze away. If Katie had suggested it, she would have turned back, but Katie trudged beside her silently. They were halfway down the walk when the door of Melanie's apartment opened, and a man appeared with a big carton in his arms.

"How did you ever manage to collect so much stuff?" he called over his shoulder. "There won't be room in the car for the three of us."

The girls heard a familiar laugh, and Melanie

ran out. Her bright hair streamed over her shoulders, and she was fairly bouncing with excitement. Her cheeks were pink, and she looked prettier than they had ever seen her.

"I'll sit on the floor," she said. "I don't care, just so I'm going home."

The man looked at her over the carton with a tender face. "Miss me, baby?"

Melanie threw her arm around his middle. "Oh, Daddy! I've missed you."

Katie tugged at Sarah's arm. "Let's go," she whispered. Sarah nodded. They began to back slowly down the walk. Melanie's father disappeared around a corner of the building, and Melanie whirled around twice as if she could hardly contain her happiness. When she caught sight of Sarah and Katie, her face changed. But an instant later she was running toward them, smiling.

"I'm going home," she called. "My father came for us, and we're going home to California."

"We know," Sarah said. "My mother told us."

Melanie flushed as if she were remembering all that had happened, but her eyes still gleamed with laughter. "I'm going home," she caroled. "I'm going home." Sarah could feel Katie, stiff and silent, beside her. There didn't seem to be anything to say. Melanie laughed right at Katie. "Aren't you glad I'm going home?" she asked.

Katie's face grew red, and her chin stuck out stubbornly, but she didn't say anything. She simply stared at Melanie until Melanie's eyes dropped. Then she said, "You were good in the play. You're a good actress," and turned and marched down the walk. Sarah looked after her, but she couldn't leave just yet.

"You were *awfully* good," she said. "And I'm glad I knew you. I hope you'll be happy at home."

For just a moment as their eyes met, Sarah saw a longing look in Melanie's, as if she wished they could really be friends. She put out her hand, and Sarah took it. But almost instantly, Melanie snatched hers away again, and laughed her mocking laugh.

"Oh, I'll be happy," she said.

She was still standing there, vivid and laughing, as Sarah turned and followed Katie.

They passed the firehouse and the corner of Fifty-seventh in silence. The air was chilly and smelled of damp, fallen leaves. An orange sunset burned in the west. Sarah remembered when they had walked this way before, and the brilliant leaves were only beginning to fall. This was the very spot on which they had quarreled. So much had happened, and Sarah felt a great deal older.

"Isn't it funny how things turn out?" she said. "When school started, I thought Miss Lane was simply perfect, and I didn't like Miss Mulkey at all. I was scared to death of Danny Wade, and I thought Wanda was perfectly silly, and . . . Oh, I've changed my mind about so many things."

"That's because you were always thinking you could tell about people from their looks."

"Well, sometimes you can," Sarah said. She was thinking of Mr. Scott, who looked nice and who was nice.

"Not really," Katie said. "You have to notice how they act. And Miss Lane never did act very nice. She wasn't one bit interested in our plays after she told us to write them."

"I know. But maybe she was thinking of something else."

"She's a schoolteacher," Katie said firmly. "She isn't supposed to be thinking of something else." She gave Sarah a sidelong look. "What do you suppose she was thinking of when she said someone had stolen her ring?"

Sarah shook her head unhappily. Katie was right, of course, but Sarah felt that there was more

to it than that. She remembered Miss Lane's sad face that morning, and how it changed when the young man came in. It was exactly as if she were a different person with the young man than she was with them. Maybe she hadn't been nice because she hadn't been happy. She said so to Katie.

Katie looked stubborn. "It doesn't matter how she felt," she said. "People can't be mean just because they're unhappy. Everyone's unhappy sometimes."

Sarah sighed. Katie was sure about things, and Sarah wasn't sure at all. Katie would put Melanie and Miss Lane right out of her mind, but Sarah knew she would think about them often, and wonder about them, and—yes—she would miss them. They were like books she hadn't finished reading. Exciting books.

"It's been interesting," she said. "I wonder if anything so interesting will ever happen again?"

Katie laughed. "Well," she said with a teasing look, "there's always the Christmas program."